HIGH HAND

A gripping cozy murder mystery full of twists

TRAUDE AILINGER

Published by The Book Folks

London, 2022

© Traude Ailinger

ISBN 978-1-80462-013-7

www.thebookfolks.com

HIGH HAND is the second standalone novel in a series of amateur sleuth mystery titles set in Edinburgh. Head to the back of this book for details about the other books.

Prologue

I never thought of myself as capable of murder, but here I am, deep in the urban canyon of the Cowgate, having just killed a man. A throng of young people, out for a boozy night, pass me. Oblivious to the rain, they laugh and shout obscenities at each other, not paying me the slightest attention. It is as if nothing has happened at all. There has been no roar of thunder, no lightning strike, no earthquake. I have committed the most heinous crime of all, broken the ultimate taboo, and yet it feels so right. The moment I struck the blow, one shard of my shattered soul slid back into place. I feel a sense of euphoria never experienced before bubbling up inside me, and I start to laugh.

I now see the law and the ten commandments for what they are: a means of controlling the plebs who would otherwise commit murder over a reduced-price sofa in IKEA. These petty rules were not meant for me. I have righted a wrong, a terrible, devastating wrong – surely that is what morality is all about? My path now lies clearly ahead, illuminated by the beaming headlights of passing cars and the pulsating neon signs above the grubby pubs and backpackers' hostels. I breathe in the damp night air and exhale deeply until my heartbeat slows. The realisation is forming gradually, like a storm cloud in a purple sky. Four more, and I will be whole again. But I have to be careful. Somehow Providence has dropped this first opportunity into my lap and sent me on my journey of recovery. From now on, I may not get away with it so easily. It is up to me to outwit the forces which will inevitably try to thwart me.

The vague outlines of a plan are beginning to form in my head when the wailing sound of approaching sirens jolt me back to the present. I sprint through the archway and melt into the darkness of a shop entrance, just before the blue lights throw their swirling patterns onto the ancient stone walls. An ambulance and a police car scream past me towards The Shamrock, and I smile. They are too late. Calmly, I walk on. I need to get ready.

Chapter 1

As always, it was with a strong sense of foreboding that Detective Inspector Russell McCord knocked on the door of Superintendent Gilchrist's office.

"Come in, come in," his boss chirped, obviously in one of his better moods.

As McCord entered, Gilchrist rose from his elevated swivel chair, a gesture clearly not in honour of McCord but for the benefit of the tall, blonde young man standing in front of his desk.

"DI McCord, may I introduce Detective Constable Duncan Calderwood, who has just joined us from Glasgow CID? Seeing that you are still one man down, I have assigned him to your team. He comes with excellent credentials and I'm sure you will make him very welcome."

The Super's tone made it clear that anything else was not an option. McCord shook the young man's hand and with one appraising glance took in his handsome features, clear hazel eyes and expensive suit. Duncan Calderwood looked as if he were destined to wear cricket whites and sip tea in a rose garden. Exactly the kind of guy you love if, like McCord, you are five feet ten and hail from a council flat in Niddrie. Calderwood could not have been out of Tulliallan Police College for more than a couple of years, and Glasgow must have been too rough a patch for his delicate constitution. Typical of the Super to land him with an upper-class chump.

"Russell McCord," was all he said by way of introduction.

"I suggest that DC Calderwood assist you with the Lamond case," the Super instructed McCord. Then he turned to the newcomer. "A suspected murder in March, still unsolved. After six months," he added pointedly.

McCord was used to Gilchrist's attempts to put him in his place but that did not make them easier to tolerate. The mutual dislike of the two men hung palpably in the air between them.

"Happy to get stuck in," Calderwood said, a little too brightly.

* * *

McCord led the way to his office along the cheerless corridor without a word, partly out of hostility, but mainly because of a natural disinclination to small talk, something he considered a waste of time. After his previous partner had gone, he had enjoyed the peace and quiet while he had the place to himself and did not relish the prospect of somebody else invading his space. At the door to his office, he turned to Calderwood whose face betrayed a mixture of anxiety and anger.

"Here we are." McCord pointed to the workstation in the far corner, empty but for a PC and an azalea fighting for survival. The plant had been a present from Amy Thornton, a journalist who fancied herself a detective and kept pestering McCord for information on current cases. With the Lamond case going nowhere, she had not been in for a while, and McCord found to his surprise that he missed her, as one might miss the noise from the flight path of an airport after moving to a quiet neighbourhood. Duncan Calderwood stood in front of the desk, clearly unwilling to sit down.

"Any questions?" McCord asked, trying to sound cordial.

Calderwood was obviously working himself up to say something, so McCord sat back in his chair and looked at him expectantly.

"I just wanted to make something clear from the start," the young man said, straightening up and jutting his chin forward. "People see my file – wealthy background, posh school, good looks – and they think: he must be a right numpty."

McCord was about to grin when he realised that this was not a boast, but rather a statement of fact. He tried to feign surprise, but realised Calderwood was having none of it when he said, "I noticed the way you looked at me in the Superintendent's office, just like the others. People treat me like a male dumb blonde; if it was a woman, they wouldn't get away with it anymore."

His face flushed, Calderwood had clearly gone off script and spat his anger in McCord's face.

"I know what you thought when the Superintendent mentioned Glasgow. 'He couldn't hack it there' – that's what you thought, wasn't it? Let me tell you what I couldn't hack. The constant put-downs from supposed colleagues. I ended up preferring the Glasgow thugs: when they don't like you, they face up to you with a knife, rather than stabbing you in the back. All I want is to be judged on merit, like everybody else."

Calderwood fell silent, seemingly deflated. McCord suspected that his new colleague was thinking that he had just made a complete prat of himself and confirmed all his boss's prejudices.

McCord's face gave nothing away.

"Duly noted," he said, suppressing a twinge of shame that he had done the same thing that he always accused others of. Calderwood suffered from the same hang-up as he did himself: constantly having to prove himself because of his background, only in reverse. Come to think of it, there was a pleasing symmetry in that.

"When the time comes – and rest assured it will – when you really get on my nerves, DC Calderwood, I promise I'll come at you from the front."

A little smile twitched around the corners of his mouth, and he saw the young man relax.

He took a thick green file from his desk and handed it to Calderwood, whose eyes lit up.

"The Lamond murder case. Sit down, for goodness' sake, and find me something in that file that I've missed."

* * *

To McCord's surprise and delight, his new sidekick did not say another word for several hours and only looked up from the file to thank McCord absent-mindedly for the coffee and chocolate bar he had brought him from the vending machine. This was an act not so much prompted by kindness, but by McCord's concern that the Super might pop in and find his protégé overworked and starving on his first day.

Eventually, Calderwood closed the file and stretched his aching back.

"So, what do you think?" McCord asked, genuinely hoping for a way out of the dead end that was this case.

"It certainly looks like murder to me," Calderwood said. "The post-mortem says–" he stopped himself. "Sorry, sir, of course you know what the PM says."

"No, no." McCord waved away his concern. "Take me through the whole thing again. I have read the files so often that I can't see the wood for the trees anymore."

Encouraged, Calderwood continued.

"The victim, Jordan Lamond, died of a severe head injury caused by a collision with the sink in the toilet of The Shamrock, an Irish pub in the Cowgate. Lamond had had a few drinks but was not particularly drunk and showed no sign of drug use. There was no indication that the floor had been slippery. The report also suggests that the head trauma was too great to have been inflicted by the impact of a mere fall, so the suspicion is that somebody grabbed Lamond by the neck or the back of the head and bashed it against the sink in one hard blow – although forensics have not come up with any foreign DNA on the body. Agreed so far?"

McCord nodded.

"Lamond's wallet, phone and watch were not taken, so robbery was not the motive. That leaves two possibilities. One: the killer was off his head with drugs and attacked a complete stranger in a fit of paranoia. Have there been any similar attacks since?"

McCord shook his head almost imperceptibly.

"Two: the killer was very angry with Mr Lamond. You quickly ruled out the man who had accompanied him to the pub, Michael somebody?"

McCord nodded again, thinking back to that day.

"Michael Sloan. He had only just taken up a job at the car dealer's where Lamond worked and wanted to make friends at the new workplace. By all accounts they got on fine. They were seen chatting and laughing minutes before Lamond went to the toilet, and a waitress is sure that Sloan did not leave his seat until the body was found shortly after by another punter. When Sloan looked into the bathroom and saw it was Lamond, his face a bloody pulp, he puked all over the floor. Forensics were delighted, of course. It wasn't him."

Calderwood agreed.

"I doubt that the attack was planned. It seems a very risky strategy to kill somebody in the toilets of a pub. Anybody could have come in and caught the attacker."

"Exactly," McCord said approvingly. "Also, according to Michael Sloan, the visit to the pub was a spontaneous decision made that same day."

"So, we have somebody who comes across Jordan Lamond in a pub, completely by chance, and who hates him so much that they bash his head in there and then."

Calderwood looked at McCord, frowning.

"They would need one hell of a motive."

"Maybe Lamond started singing Irish ballads," McCord suggested.

Calderwood grinned.

"But seriously, we checked Lamond's phone, emails and all written correspondence. We interviewed pretty much everybody he was in touch with the year leading up to his murder and we found nothing. He was a bit of a loser. Went to Edinburgh University, your alma mater, too, I believe," McCord said with a wink, "but only scraped through his degree. A so-called gap year afterwards, in Vietnam, before trying to make the big bucks with a consultancy firm working five hours a week. Unsurprisingly, this failed, and after a few other attempts at commercial success, Daddy had enough of bailing out his son and gave him a choice: either all his allowances cancelled or work properly in the family's car dealership. Sensibly, if grudgingly, Lamond took the latter option, and the relationship between him and his parents finally began to improve. Occasional gambling, recreational drug use, one caution for drunken and disorderly behaviour and a few speeding tickets; all in all, your average customer of The Shamrock."

"Girlfriends?"

"Nothing serious, apart from one who broke up with him before he took the car salesman job. He tried to get back together with her afterwards, but she was already in another relationship. There was no sign of unusual bitterness or him stalking her. The impression I got was that nobody really cared enough about the guy to spend a lot of time with him, let alone kill him."

"The CCTV was inconclusive?"

"Yes, somebody left the pub through the back door, very soon after the attack must have happened. An average-sized figure, probably male, in trousers and hoodie, stooping and then running off. If that was the killer, he must have had blood on him, but we could find no witnesses who saw him outside. It was dark and raining at the time. Nobody apart from the usual cranks came forward."

"Well, I can't think of anything else either." Calderwood sounded annoyed with himself.

"Maybe it was simply a crackhead," McCord said. "Maybe he was so horrified at what the drugs made him do that he went into rehab and has become a respectable citizen atoning for his sins by working in some charity or other, and we will never see him again."

Of course, he did not believe that for a minute.

"That would be lovely," Calderwood said with a grimace. "But then we would never find out, would we? And I hate not finding out. Shall I go back further in time into Lamond's background and see if I can find someone with an old grudge?"

McCord smiled. "You do that. But tomorrow will do."

He was turning out to be not too bad after all, this Calderwood.

Chapter 2

On Monday morning, Amy Thornton was woken up by her phone buzzing and bouncing on her bedside table like a demented bumblebee. Bleary-eyed, she unlocked the screen. After reading a couple of messages, she jumped out of bed. Something was going on at Dunsapie Loch, and it sounded like the story she desperately needed for the next edition of the magazine. She had a quick wash, hastily put on cotton twill trousers and a lambswool jumper and brushed her long, black hair. She wondered if DI McCord would be at the scene. If it was a murder, the chances were good. Since the McAdie case, he tolerated her at the station where she occasionally picked up a useful lead. In return, she shared any information she gained freely with him and gave him the benefit of her ideas, although she felt they were not always fully appreciated.

With her hair coiled up and fixed with her favourite Celtic clasp, she slipped on her calf-leather boots. Normally, it was just as fast walking in the centre of town as driving, but it was early, and she needed to get there before the other hacks.

"I'm taking the car, Mum!" she shouted across the hall, picking her way through removal boxes, a half-naked mannequin and black plastic bags full of clothes. Not giving her mother much of a chance to protest, she picked the car keys from the hook by the door and was off.

* * *

At the same time, McCord was on the tortuous journey from Portobello into the centre of Edinburgh, cursing the traffic as he did every morning, when his mobile rang.

"Morning, sir." He recognized the duty sergeant's voice. "Someone has reported a body found on Queen's Drive, just south of Dunsapie Loch. You might want to go straight there. SOCO are on their way."

"Thanks, Jack. When DC Calderwood appears, send him out there as well."

He rang off and looked at the seemingly endless line of cars crawling along Portobello Road. There would be no time for birdwatching on the loch but with a bit of luck, he would get to the crime scene before the corpse had completely decomposed.

* * *

McCord weaved his way through the small crowd that had gathered outside the blue and white crime scene tape. People jostled for position and held their phones high, hoping for a picture to liven up their social media accounts. It was still early but quite a few joggers were out on their morning circuit round Queen's Drive. He showed his ID to the constable guarding the perimeter and ducked under the tape. A small white tent had been erected on the road, and McCord was not looking forward to what he would see in there.

The SOCOs were still busy preparing the walkway and taking photographs, so McCord put on the blue plastic overshoes and gloves and took in the immediate surroundings while he was waiting. Queen's Drive was a narrow, tarmacked road circling Arthur's Seat, and a popular route for joggers and dog walkers. This particular stretch was lined by shrubs whose golden and bronze leaves would provide decent enough cover for an attacker, especially in the dark. A bright orange sun had just risen above the horizon. It seemed unnaturally huge to McCord, as if it had moved closer to see what was going on.

"DI McCord!"

McCord turned at the familiar voice. Among the onlookers, he could not make her out; only when she had pushed her way through to the front did Amy Thornton's petite, slim figure emerge from the crowd.

"What's going on?" she asked without preamble.

"That's what I'm trying to find out, Miss Thornton, and I'll get there quicker if I'm not harassed with questions while going about my job."

Despite the formal address and his impatient tone, his eyes smiled. Somehow a case would not be a case if Amy Thornton did not stick her long nose into it.

One of the SOCOs waved him over, so McCord walked towards the tent, opened the flap and entered.

"Morning, Dr Crane," McCord greeted the pathologist, and thought once again how ill-fitting names could be. Dumpy, extremely short-legged and seemingly devoid of a neck, the pathologist should have a name like Coot instead, which would also have taken account of the white hair flattened on his head.

"What have we got?"

Crane looked bored and disappointed as usual. McCord suspected he nourished the hope of a bizarre ritual murder conducted in extreme temperatures involving exotic poisons and obscure instruments that would finally challenge his well-known expertise. But this was not it. He struggled to his feet and peeled off his stained latex gloves.

"Male, bludgeoned to death with a stone at 7.28am."

He lifted two clear plastic bags, one containing a fist-sized rock, covered in the victim's blood, the other a watch, its face shattered.

"Severe trauma at the back of the head that would have killed him instantly."

McCord always started at the feet of a corpse, working his way up slowly to the more unpleasant bits. The trainers looked like a size fifteen and McCord guessed they had cost more than his own suit. The rest of the body, clad in a stylish charcoal jogging outfit, reminded him of a stranded whale, seeming even more massive because it was lying completely still. His eyes did not linger on the congealing, maroon mass that used to be the back of the victim's skull but swiftly moved on to focus on the misshapen ear that stuck out at almost a right angle, defying the destruction right next to it.

"Rugby player?" McCord wondered aloud.

"Robert 'Battering Ram' McArthur, thirty-two years old. Second Row in the Scotland team until four years ago when he was banned for a series of dangerous and illegal tackles, hence the nickname. Owner of the gym New You."

McCord looked up in surprise.

"His wallet with a business card," Crane explained. "And you clearly don't follow the rugby."

"More a football man, myself," McCord admitted.

"Well, I'm off to finish my breakfast that was so rudely interrupted," Crane announced. "I'll send you the post-mortem asap but don't get your hopes up. Not much of a mystery here."

"But how?" McCord was baffled. "How did they manage to sneak up on him and hit him on the back of the head with such force? And why?"

The pathologist shrugged.

"That's your problem, not mine. Oh, I almost forgot: SOCO found a cigarette stub behind the bush there; it's dry on top. It rained last night, so someone must have dropped it this morning. Maybe the killer was waiting for the victim to jog past. You might be looking for a big, not very friendly giant with a smoking habit who is not very concerned about leaving evidence behind. Or somebody who is awfully good at shot put. Should be wrapped up soon." He looked resentful. "I wish murderers these days would make a little more of an effort."

With a last irritated wave of his right hand, he departed.

* * *

McCord stepped out of the tent to find DC Calderwood standing at the entrance, his notebook open and looking at him expectantly.

"Morning, sir."

McCord just nodded.

"You missed all the fun. Want a look?"

He half expected Calderwood to decline his offer and defer to Dr Crane's expertise, but he was wrong. Without a word, Calderwood ducked into the entrance. After a few minutes he came out, and McCord noticed with some satisfaction that the normally healthy glow of his DC's skin was tinged with green.

"Are you okay?" McCord asked, because he felt he had to.

"Absolutely fine," Calderwood insisted. "Do we know anything about the victim apart from the fact that he consumed far too much protein?"

McCord filled him in, and Calderwood shared his confusion about the how and why.

"We need to interview the witness who found the body," McCord said. "Maybe they can shed a light."

"Done that already, sir." Calderwood flicked back the pages in his notebook. "A Miss Eilidh Gordon, out for a jog. She says in the twilight she wasn't sure at first what was lying on the path ahead of her. When she realised it was a body, she called the emergency services immediately. The call was recorded at 7.41am. She is quite sure she has not seen the victim before; she didn't have a closer look, understandably, but says she would have remembered the size of him. She didn't notice anybody around at that time but if McArthur was killed at 7.28am, the attacker had plenty time to disappear, on foot or by car without being seen. Not many people are keen, or daft, enough to jog before sunrise." He looked up. "Is there anything else you want to ask her, sir? Otherwise, we can let her go home. She's pretty shaken up."

McCord shook his head.

"Not at the moment."

He considered adding a nurturing 'Well done, Calderwood,' but decided it would be patronising.

They had reached the perimeter where the small crowd had grown to a substantial throng, augmented by members of the press. They recognised McCord from previous cases and started shouting questions at him.

McCord cleared his throat.

"If you know or have witnessed anything relating to this incident, please speak to any of the officers here. If not, please move along. There will be an official statement later today."

The last few words of the sentence were drowned out by the engine noise of the ambulance that took the body away. A constable untied some of the tape to let it pass. McCord and Calderwood stepped aside, only to bump into Amy Thornton, who was still hovering around.

"Any idea who the body is?" she asked.

"Who says there is a body?" McCord grunted, aware of other people listening and having learned the hard way to leave *all* public statements to Superintendent Gilchrist.

Amy rolled her eyes.

"Don't insult my intelligence, McCord. The ambulance drivers carried a stretcher out of a crime scene tent – a stretcher that was completely covered."

"Well, then draw your own conclusions," McCord retorted.

Only now did he notice the expectant gaze with which Calderwood eyed Amy.

"DC Calderwood, this is Amy Thornton, a journalist with the magazine *Forth Write*. She assisted us in a previous inquiry." He turned to Amy. "DC Calderwood has just joined Edinburgh CID from Glasgow."

"Pleased to meet you." Discreetly appraising Calderwood's face and worsted suit, she shook his hand with a mischievous grin. "It is nice to see that they found a new partner at last for DI McCord."

Calderwood managed a non-committal smile. "I count myself lucky to be working with DI McCord," he said.

McCord maintained a deadpan expression. "You have just demonstrated a serious lack of judgement, DC Calderwood," McCord said. "But never mind, you'll learn."

With a knowing laugh, Amy discreetly motioned the men away from the crime scene until they could not be overheard by any of the onlookers.

"Just give me a name, McCord," she pleaded, "so I know where to start. I promise I won't breathe a syllable until it is official."

McCord knew she would not and that with her unique ability to draw confidences out of unsuspecting people, she might well be useful to the investigation. But he also knew that sharing confidential information with a journalist was against the rules, and if Gilchrist found out, there would be hell to pay. Calderwood seemed a decent enough guy, but they had only met the previous day, and it was far too early to trust him.

"You know I can't do that," McCord replied with a side glance to Calderwood. "But no doubt our Superintendent will be giving a public statement very soon."

Amy pulled a face.

"You're such a stickler for procedure, McCord," she said. "But never mind. I bet you ten quid that I find the killer first!"

Both men watched her slight, elegant back melt into the crowd. McCord was the first to remember why they were here in the first place.

Calderwood was still staring at the gap in the crowd. "Wow," was all he said.

McCord was not sure why he did not like this comment. But now it was time to visit the grieving relatives and to find out who had reason to despatch Robert McArthur into the next world in such a decisive manner.

* * *

The station had gone quiet, but McCord was not ready to go home yet. The first twenty-four hours of an investigation were crucial, and they had not made any real progress despite having spent a full day researching Robert McArthur's family life and business. McCord was reading over the statement of Robert McArthur's widow Olivia who had been devastated at the news of his death and been left in the care of a family liaison officer until a relative could be found to look after her and the baby. She had no idea why anybody would want to harm her husband. According to McArthur's mother, Robert and Olivia had been a devoted couple. The neighbours had seen them kiss goodbye the morning he was killed and had confirmed that Olivia had not left the house until the police turned up to inform her of his death. There was a modest life insurance, but McCord did not think she had anything to do with the murder.

According to Olivia McArthur, Robert had spent the weekend grouse shooting with a group of old friends up at Carnethy Estate. McCord would go up there first thing in the morning.

Calderwood had also declined to clock off, poring over the statements of the gym staff, hoping to find any contradictions, signs of illegal performance-enhancing drugs or other misdeeds. When the phone rang, both men looked up hopefully, but it was only the desk sergeant telling McCord that Miss Thornton was on her way up.

"For a journalist, she has easy access to the station, hasn't she?" Calderwood observed.

"Amy isn't one of the usual hacks" – McCord sounded more defensive than he had intended to – "and she helped solve the McAdie case."

"I heard about that one," Calderwood said excitedly. "Wasn't she the one who…"

He did not finish his sentence as Amy Thornton entered the office, tired but buoyed by the hope of finding out something new.

"DI McCord, DC Calderwood," she said by way of a greeting. "Anything new?"

Her knowing little smile told McCord that she had guessed the answer correctly.

"I couldn't find anything at McArthur's gym either," Amy said casually.

"So, you went there as well, did you?" McCord still could not get used to her undisguised meddling in his investigations.

"Beat you to it," Amy said triumphantly, "despite having to wait until Superintendent Gilchrist made his statement. People are less guarded with clients than they are with the police. I was at the gym for two hours, given an introduction by my new personal trainer, instructions on how to use the machines and a one-hour session. They won't be happy if I cancel my subscription tomorrow, but I reckon it was for a good cause. The PT told me that the duty manager phoned McArthur at home when he didn't turn up and didn't answer his mobile, and his wife told him he had been murdered. He and the staff were genuinely shocked and sad. He was well enough liked, by the sounds of it. Of course, if the murderer was one of the staff, he or she would not have been at work this morning. But nobody said anything about any animosities."

McCord nodded.

"We had the same impression when we interviewed them."

Calderwood, clearly keen to make an impression, opened his mouth. "We might find out something tomorrow morning. We're going to–"

"We're going to talk to some friends of McArthur's," McCord interrupted. "Hopefully, that will give us a lead. But now it's time to get some rest. It'll be a long day tomorrow."

Amy eyed McCord suspiciously but did not press him further.

"Ok, I'll let you know if I find anything else. And can I just say, the way you treat my plant should be a criminal offence."

And with that she sailed out of the office.

McCord was annoyed.

"I've watered that damn plant every day," he grumbled.

Calderwood lifted the azalea out of the pot by the stem to reveal a sodden, mouldy mass of tangled roots and soil.

"You've drowned it," Calderwood observed. "Happens a lot with people who mean well but don't know anything about plants."

"I'm a homicide detective, not a bloody gardener," McCord snapped.

Quickly, Calderwood changed the subject.

"Why didn't you want her to know about us going to the Carnethy Estate tomorrow?" he asked. "Maybe she could have come along–"

"Because," McCord cut him short, "the friend Robert McArthur was staying with on Carnethy Estate is a certain Andrew Campbell who has an older brother, John Campbell. And John Campbell is not only the owner of *Forth Write* magazine and therefore Amy's boss, but also the boyfriend of her mother. I'd like to have a chat with Andrew Campbell before Miss Thornton figures that out. As soon as she does, she *will* get involved, and with her connection to the family, she might prove to be very useful to the investigation."

Chapter 3

The narrow road leading up to Carnethy House wound its way through rolling hills and the occasional pine wood. The sky was overcast but the rain would hold off until later. The pungent smell from burning heather wafted across the rolling hills, rusty brown now that its purple glory had faded. McCord loved the fragrant melancholy of the autumn, the last burst of colour and fruitfulness before the bleak and brutal winter.

"Just half an hour away from the centre, and it's a different world," Calderwood remarked as he lowered his window and inhaled. His lungs, accustomed to exhaust fumes saturating the morning air, went into spasm, and he coughed.

"Been too long in the city, eh?" McCord grinned. "Did you not grow up on a posh estate like this?"

"Not quite," Calderwood answered, sounding annoyed at being pulled up on his privileged upbringing. "We lived in a comfortable house, true, but my father is a QC, not a landowner, and he has worked very hard for his money."

"Well, my father is an electrician, and he has worked very hard all his life trying to pay the bills for his not so comfortable council flat," McCord batted back.

"We can't choose the life we are born into, but we can choose what we make of it," Calderwood said.

Although secretly McCord entirely agreed with Calderwood, he gave a little snort. "You are very wise for your age; maybe you should have become a judge after all."

When Calderwood said nothing, McCord added in a more conciliatory tone, "for what it's worth, I think you'll make a fine DI one day."

"Thanks." Calderwood sounded surprised and gratified, and they drove on in companionable silence.

McCord was scanning the horizon for birds of prey. Last time he had been up in the Pentlands birdwatching, he had seen a merlin cruising low above the heather, but he could detect no movement anywhere. The grey skies were empty. No wonder, McCord thought angrily, if they shoot at anything that moves and poison predators that might eat their precious grouse. He had no evidence of the Campbells doing this, but he was predisposed to suspect landowners of the worst crimes against the bird world.

"So, what do we know about this Andrew Campbell?" Calderwood asked eventually.

"Thirty-two years old, son of Mrs Edith Campbell, who owns the estate. A few speeding and parking tickets, one drink-driving charge a few years ago. Andrew Campbell, not his mother. She, apparently, is a paragon of upper-class rectitude."

"You said you know his brother? John Campbell, was it?"

"Right. Met him while on the McAdie case." Remembering that Calderwood hailed from the upper echelons of society, he chose his words carefully. "Seemed a decent enough guy. He was in love with Amy's mother, Valerie Thornton, and very protective of Amy. She bagged exclusive interviews with the people involved in the McAdie case and ran a feature over several weeks."

"I didn't have you down as a reader of magazines," Calderwood said.

"I bought the issues with the articles about the case," McCord said dismissively, failing to add that he had enjoyed them immensely. "The serialisation of the story gave *Forth Write* a new lease of life. But that was six months ago, so Amy will be desperate now for another scoop."

"Awkward, though, if a family member is involved, isn't it?" Calderwood remarked.

"Exactly," McCord agreed. "Let's hope he isn't."

* * *

Carnethy House was built in the latter part of the nineteenth century by John and Andrew Campbell's great-great grandfather who had made his fortune producing tobacco in the colonies and importing it into Great Britain, thereby spreading both abject misery and disease across the globe. Conical roofs and tourelles topped massive grey ashlar stone walls set at bizarre angles. It all seemed to have been thrown together by chance rather than design and made it look like something out of a fairy tale, enchanting and menacing at the same time. The trees surrounding the house had been planted at the time it was built and now formed a protective circle against the weather and the outside world.

McCord had wondered if he should announce his visit and weighed up the advantage of catching everybody off guard against the disadvantage of antagonising one of Edinburgh's grand families, which would not please Superintendent Gilchrist at all. There was also the possibility of not finding Andrew Campbell at home and wasting precious time. In the end, he had phoned the office and been lucky. An employee had informed him that both Mr and Mrs Campbell were at home and were not expected to leave the estate that morning. Without stating his title or business, McCord had told the man that he would pay them a visit at ten o'clock and hung up.

As they drove through a magnificent set of wrought-iron gates flanked by a low stone wall, they saw a short, upright figure descending the stairs leading up to the main entrance.

"That must be Mrs Campbell," McCord said. "Strange, I thought they'd have a butler and a row of curtsying maids waiting for us."

"Times are hard for some of these estates," Calderwood remarked. "The upkeep of such a pile costs millions, and while the owners are asset-rich, they're often cash-poor."

"My heart bleeds," was all McCord said as his Nissan Juke crunched to a halt on the pink gravel of the yard.

The detectives made their way towards Mrs Campbell who was waiting for them at the bottom of the stairs. McCord pulled out a small leather wallet that he flicked open with practised ease.

"Good morning. I am Detective Inspector McCord from Edinburgh CID; this is Detective Constable Calderwood. Mrs Edith Campbell?"

She nodded and reluctantly offered her cool hand. McCord felt a chill emanating from this woman whose steel-grey hair blended into the stone behind and the leaden sky above her. There was no warmth in the dark eyes scrutinizing him, but she had the easy and gracious smile that becomes second nature in a lifetime of entertaining and keeping up a façade.

"Apologies for calling on you at such short notice, ma'am," Calderwood made up for his boss's curtness, "but there is no need to be alarmed. We are just making routine enquiries into the death of Mr Robert McArthur, and we were told that he spent last weekend here."

Her hand moved up to her pearl necklace and fingered it as if it were a rosary.

"Robbie McArthur is dead? Oh dear." Her lowered voice and tone were perfectly appropriate for such news, and yet McCord had the distinct feeling that her only concern was how this might affect herself and her family. "Please, come in."

She led the way up the steps into a grand hall decorated with old weapons, paintings of dubious quality portraying what were bound to be ancestors, and stuffed stags' heads. From the opposite wall, a gentleman with a benevolent smile was looking down on them.

"My dear, departed husband, Kenneth Campbell," Edith Campbell said when McCord hesitated in front of the picture.

McCord was struck by the family resemblance in Kenneth and John Campbell. Having now met Edith Campbell, he had some idea why John had given up the estate with all its grandeur and acres of wild moor for the magazine and his relatively modest flat in George Street.

"It can't be easy running the estate on your own," Calderwood remarked with sympathy.

"Oh, I'm not on my own," she hastily corrected him as if she resented the pity concealed in his remark. "My son Andrew runs the estate now with the help of an estate manager."

A young woman in jeans and sweatshirt carrying a bucket appeared from a small door behind the impressive mahogany staircase.

"Ah, Lucy, bring some tea into the drawing room," Edith Campbell commanded. She turned to her visitors. "Or would you prefer coffee?"

"Coffee, please," Calderwood and McCord said simultaneously.

"You heard, Lucy, and be quick about it."

The girl scuttled off.

"Lucy does some cleaning for us several days a week," Edith Campbell explained, trying not to sound mortified at the implication that they could not afford a full-time housemaid. "I must apologise for her poor attire and attitude. When she first applied for the job, she seemed such a cheerful, pretty girl. Always well turned-out. And after only a week, she turned into an ogre." Mrs Campbell sighed. "One just can't get the staff these days. Please, come in and have a seat."

The drawing room looked out over the back garden that must have been splendid in the past but had turned wild with neglect. Somebody had savagely pruned the shrubs and mowed the lawn but clearly had no further ambitions in terms of gardening. McCord gazed out of the window, thinking of the wonderful habitat the untidy garden provided for ground nesting birds, when Edith Campbell invited them to sit down on the flowery sofa.

"My son Andrew will be down in a minute," she said, "but I'm not sure how we can help you. Surely, all this has nothing to do with us."

An odd statement considering she doesn't even know what 'this' is, thought McCord, or does she? McArthur's name had not been released to the press until this morning.

"I am told Robert McArthur visited you over the weekend," he said instead.

"He did," Edith Campbell confirmed. "He and a couple of other friends Andrew knows from his time at Edinburgh University."

"What a coincidence," Calderwood butted in, "both DI McCord and I are alumni as well."

Edith Campbell threw a quick glance at McCord's cheap suit.

"How extraordinary," was all she managed to say.

"Did you know Mr McArthur well?" McCord enquired, trying to control a rising irritation.

"Ach, you know, young people now have no interest in our generation, so when they come, I just have dinner with them and then leave them to it."

She was clearly pleased with her deep insight into the psyche of others and her boundless generosity of spirit.

"Did anything unusual happen during their stay?" asked McCord.

"Well–"

She was interrupted by her son, who breezed into the room with a big smile.

"Mama, won't you introduce me to our guests?"

She waved her hand as if he did not need an introduction and the visitors did not merit one but humoured them, nevertheless.

"This is my son Andrew. Andrew, this is..." she faltered, not remembering their names.

"DI McCord and DC Calderwood from Edinburgh CID," McCord said, heaving himself out of the sofa.

Andrew Campbell shook their hands enthusiastically and made a show of being worried.

"I haven't been caught speeding again, have I?" he joked. "Although I doubt that they would bring in the big guns for that."

He flopped into an armchair with his legs apart; the picture of a man with nothing to hide. His carefully combed hair was still damp, and McCord concluded that

Mama had chased him out of bed just as they had arrived.

Lucy arrived with a tray almost too heavy for her to carry and without either of the Campbells stirring, she set it down on the coffee table with a relieved thump.

"Thank you, Lucy, you'd better get on with your work now," Edith Campbell told her, as if serving drinks was a privilege rather than a chore.

McCord remembered John Campbell making coffee for him and Amy's mother in her small shop in the spring and marvelled at how different brothers could be. Andrew had the finer, more chiselled features of his mother and the good looks found in male models for expensive outfitters, but a weak chin and a charming smile that McCord suspected was entirely artificial.

"The detectives say that Robbie McArthur is dead," Edith Campbell informed her son while she was pouring coffee into tiny porcelain cups.

"What?" Andrew exclaimed, straightening up. "Our Robbie? I don't believe it. What happened? A car accident?"

"Surely, detectives would not come to interrogate us if it had been a mere accident," his mother observed while handing out steaming cups and passing round a plate with biscuits.

"Nobody is being interrogated," McCord said. He could already hear the Super's voice warning him to act with more sensitivity. "We are just trying to establish what happened in the run-up to his death."

He felt Calderwood wince at the unfortunate turn of phrase.

"So how did he die?" Andrew asked.

McCord took a sip of his coffee.

"He was hit on the back of the head with a rock while he was out jogging," he said, watching Andrew closely.

"I don't believe it," Andrew said again. The cup in his hand wobbled dangerously on the saucer, so he put it down. "Why would anybody do that?"

"That's what we're trying to find out. Did he say anything about feeling threatened? Can you think of anybody who might have reason to kill him?"

"Absolutely not." Andrew was emphatic. "He was such a nice chap. Poor Olivia, she must be devastated."

"Who else was here last weekend?" McCord asked as Calderwood flipped open his notebook.

"Just a couple of university friends of ours. Alexander Buchan and Zacharias Walker. They both live in Edinburgh. They arrived for dinner on Friday, around seven. On Saturday we went grouse shooting, and afterwards we played some cards, blackjack and poker, although it is not much fun with just four people."

McCord noticed that Edith Campbell's lips had tightened to a thin line.

"High stakes?" he asked.

"No chance." Andrew laughed. "Just enough in the tin for a meal next time we go out in Edinburgh."

"Do you often see each other?"

"They come up a couple of times a year, and sometimes we meet in the town for an evening out. Always good, clean fun."

Andrew Campbell took another sip of coffee.

"Was it common knowledge that Mr McArthur went jogging around Arthur's Seat before sunrise?" McCord asked.

"Oh yes," Andrew said, sombre again. "He had a thing about fitness. He tried to persuade Alex and Zac to take up jogging, but they were having none of it. Do you know that Robbie owned a gym in town?"

"We do." McCord watched Andrew Campbell's face closely. "Where were you this morning around seven thirty?" he suddenly added.

"Surely, you can't think that *my* son…" Edith Campbell's voice choked with indignation at the mere suggestion.

"This is just routine," Calderwood butted in hastily. "We have to ask everybody whose name comes up in an investigation if they have an alibi. A pure formality, I can assure you."

Andrew Campbell set down his cup calmly.

"It's all right, Mama. The detectives are just doing their job." He looked McCord straight in the eye. "I'm afraid, I am rather a late riser. I would still be fast asleep at half seven."

"And I can vouch for that," Edith Campbell snapped. "I woke him up around ten. I take it your business is finished here?"

"Indeed. For now," McCord added, simply to annoy her.

He drained his cup with one gulp and rose to his feet. Calderwood, regretfully eyeing his half-finished coffee, hastily stood up.

"Well, thank you, we won't take up any more of your time. Please let me know if anything else comes to mind later." He dropped his card on the tray. "Goodbye, Mrs Campbell," he said and followed Andrew towards the hall.

Calderwood gave a slight bow. "Thank you for the coffee, Mrs Campbell."

The cloud cover had thinned to allow a few pale strips of blue to emerge. Bundled rays of sunshine pointed like fingers on various spots on the lawn and the wilderness beyond.

On their way to the car, Andrew supplied the easy, polite conversation about nothing in particular, which McCord always regarded as the main benefit of an expensive education, apart from forming useful business connections, of course, that led you straight into the upper echelons of society. When they reached the Juke, McCord politely waited for Andrew to finish his sentence about the ghastly traffic in Edinburgh.

Sliding into the driver's seat, he asked casually, "Oh, just one more thing. Do you smoke, Mr Campbell?"

Taken aback, Andrew hesitated. "I'm afraid, I do," he said eventually with a little laugh. "Sadly, it is one of my many vices."

"A very unhealthy one, or so I'm told. Goodbye, Mr Campbell," McCord said, pulled the door shut and drove off watching Andrew in the rear-view mirror. The manager of Carnethy Estate watched the car move away and then took out his phone.

Calderwood grinned.

"Nicely done, sir. Watched Columbo in your youth as well?"

"Who?" McCord asked, absent-mindedly, thinking ahead to the interviews with the other men who had been there last weekend.

His train of thought was interrupted by frantic bleeping from the Juke's onboard computer. Muttering under his breath, he put on his seat belt and sped towards the city.

Chapter 4

A little later that morning, John Campbell called Amy into his office.

"The McArthur murder you have been working on–" he began when they had both sat down.

"Yes," Amy interrupted, frustration in her voice. "I've already seen DI McCord. He is working the case, but he hasn't given me anything useful yet. Mind you, I suspect they haven't got very far, as usual, so I'm working on background on social media."

"Well, there is now an added complication to the case," John said, looking worried. "My mother has just phoned to tell me that the police have been on the estate. Apparently, the victim was a university friend of Andrew's and spent the weekend with him there."

Amy's dark eyebrows contracted while she was taking this in.

"You don't seriously think your brother could have anything to do with the murder?" she asked.

"Of course not," John said, hastily. "On the other hand, Andrew has not been exactly a model citizen. If the police dig into his affairs, I wonder what they will find. Also, we must be very careful what we print about the case. I am going up later to speak to him."

"I'll come with you," Amy declared before John could make another suggestion. "Four eyes see more than two. And I can distract your mother, while you have a quiet word with Andrew."

John sighed.

"I just hope that he has not got himself mixed up in something nasty this time."

* * *

McCord made for the desk of DC Heather 'The Hacker' Sutton, so named by her colleagues for her incomparable computer skills. Nobody would have called her this to her face, but then again, people rarely talked to DC Sutton at all. Usually, only McCord was brave enough to venture near her workstation.

She told McCord in her inimitable way that she had not yet found any irregularities in Robert McArthur's financial records.

"Nothing yet, I'll let you know." Which was her way of saying 'bugger off and let me get on with my job'. DC Sutton lacked even the most basic people skills but proved invaluable when information needed to be retrieved legitimately from bank accounts and business records, or, on occasion, from that grey zone that was usually inhabited by criminals. Since she had helped solve the McAdie case, McCord often gave her tasks that needed exceptional skills as well as discretion. Each time, however, he tried not to think what would happen if DC Sutton went over to the dark side.

* * *

Back in his office, McCord went over to Calderwood. "Anything on our chummy foursome?" he asked.

Calderwood looked up from his computer screen, eyes bright with excitement.

"Alexander Buchan, Andrew Campbell's friend who was at the weekend shoot, is on the system. Arrested for breach of the peace and assault on, wait for it, Robert McArthur, eleven years ago, during their final year at uni. Apparently, there was a love triangle involving a girl, Cheryl Langley. During the brawl, Buchan accused McArthur of behaving 'like a complete cad' towards the girl whom he was in love with. McArthur didn't file any charges and was keen to blame the whole incident on an excessive amount of rum being consumed during one of their poker games. Buchan repented and got off with a caution. Not even a parking ticket since then."

"Well, well," McCord said. "Let's go and ask Mr Buchan himself about his friend Robert McArthur."

At the door, he turned round.

"Well done, DC Calderwood. Good work."

* * *

Alexander Buchan lived in a spacious Victorian semi out in Cramond. He was having dinner with his wife when the inspectors called but did not mind at all answering a few questions regarding 'poor Robbie'. He had difficulty taking this in, he told McCord. Robbie had always been so full of life. He'd seen him only two days ago after a lovely weekend shooting, playing cards and enjoying dinner – it was impossible to think he was no longer alive. And poor Olivia, what must she be going through? Buchan's wife took his hand in hers in a show of marital support and affection.

"Indeed," McCord said, cutting through the clichés. "I take it then that the pair of you have made up since you assaulted him for the way he treated Cheryl Langley?"

Alexander Buchan was clearly rattled at this unexpected turn of questioning. His wife withdrew her hand.

"But that is ancient history!" he exclaimed.

"Hmm." McCord made a show of looking Buchan up and down. "Very brave of you to attack somebody of Mr McArthur's stature. You must have been either very drunk, or very, very angry."

Buchan was beginning to perspire.

"Jealousy and too much drink can make young men do stupid things. We are, eh, we were friends, Robbie and I. All water under the bridge."

"Are you still in contact with Cheryl?" McCord asked, although the answer was obvious with the wife sitting right there.

"Not since then. Nothing at all."

"I'm not sure what you are angling at," Mrs Buchan said. "What has all this to do with poor Robbie's murder? You're not suggesting Alex killed him because of a drunken fight years ago?"

"Just building up a picture," McCord said calmly. "Such questions are routine in a murder inquiry. Where were you yesterday morning around seven thirty, Mr Buchan?"

Alexander Buchan looked decidedly uncomfortable now.

"I had a call for an early viewing of a property in Marchmont but when I got there, the client didn't turn up. I went straight to the office afterwards."

"Can anybody confirm that, Mr Buchan?"

"I'm afraid not. I was in the car on my own, and my staff did not come into the office until eight thirty."

"Pity," McCord remarked, unconvincingly. "Well, unless there is something else you want to tell me, we'll be on our way. Please get in touch if you remember anything that might be pertinent to our inquiry."

McCord rose from the armchair, and his DC followed him outside, leaving behind a very nervous husband and a wife bursting with questions about a former girlfriend she had known nothing about.

"Don't you think you were a bit hard on him, sir?" Calderwood ventured when his boss pulled away from the kerb. "His wife is right – it seems unlikely that their fight had anything to do with the murder."

"He's hiding something," McCord replied, watching the traffic ahead. "And he'll need to change his shirt now, if not his underpants."

But he knew as well as Calderwood that he simply enjoyed putting the wind up a murder suspect.

Chapter 5

Amy leaned back in the passenger seat of John's eight-year-old Audi and thought about her boss, who in the last six months had become like a father to her. John was not the type to inflict his emotions on the people around him, but Amy could tell that he was deeply concerned. While he refused even to contemplate the possibility of Andrew's involvement in the murder, they could not be sure at all that Andrew had not done some shady dealings on the fringes of it. Any hint of that would no doubt be unearthed by DI McCord and possibly by Amy herself.

Since her sensational revelations about the McAdie case, the magazine's readers were now expecting more of the same. This potential conflict of interest was bound to make John uneasy. Amy fervently hoped that Andrew could provide a watertight alibi and that he had nothing to do with whoever had murdered his university friend. She now saw it as her mission to find out everything Andrew might have done before McCord did and to prevent the detective from jumping to conclusions. She considered McCord a friend, sort of, and had the impression that he liked John, but she was sure he would cheerfully put the handcuffs on Andrew if he thought that he was a murderer.

As they drove through the imposing gates and approached Carnethy House, Amy experienced the mixture of awe and envy that it was meant to inspire in those visiting it for the first time. In a way, it was strange that neither she nor her mother had been introduced to John's family yet, when Valerie was just about to sell her flat and move in with him. When Amy had asked him about it, he had said that he was reluctant to subject them to his mother's snobbery. Amy looked across to John, whose features had hardened in anticipation of the impending meeting, and silently vowed to make a good first impression on his mother.

* * *

Edith Campbell had been on the lookout for her older son and awaited them on the steps. She presented a cool cheek to be kissed and then turned to Amy.

"I didn't know you were bringing a guest?" she rebuked her son, while taking in Amy's elegant outfit, her confident bearing and the dark complexion that gave her a slightly exotic look.

"Mama, this is Amy Thornton. She works with me on the magazine and has kindly agreed to help."

With what, he wisely omitted, since his mother would be resentful enough to have a stranger around during a family crisis.

"It's a pleasure to meet you, Mrs Campbell," Amy said and shook a hand whose light touch she suspected was deceptive. "John and I will do everything we can to support Andrew and keep the story out of the papers."

"As far as I am concerned, there *is* no story," Edith Campbell said pointedly.

"Well, let's make sure of that," John answered drily. "Shall we go in?"

* * *

When they entered the drawing room, Andrew had already helped himself to coffee and a biscuit, but seeing there was a young lady present, he got up with alacrity and greeted Amy with barely disguised curiosity which grew into grudging admiration as the conversation progressed. After he had recounted the meeting with the detectives in detail, but without the venom exhibited by his mother, he poured himself another cup.

The old-fashioned phone rang in the hall, and Lucy announced that Lady Smythe-Tennyson was asking to speak with Mrs Campbell.

As Edith hurried outside to take the call, Amy shot a surprised glance at John. Phoebe Smythe-Tennyson was a good friend of John's and had helped to promote Valerie's designs among her friends in the nobility.

There was only a trace of a smile around John's eyes. "I think we can speak more freely without Mama present," he said, turning to his brother. "And now tell us what you did not tell the police. Anything we should know about your friends and your dealings with them?" John asked.

Andrew shrugged. "There is really nothing to tell. We only see each other several times a year for a general catch-up. We had the usual, pleasant dinner with Mama on the Friday, a shoot and card games on the Saturday, dinner again, and then they all went off after a late breakfast on Sunday morning. I have no idea why this detective – McCord, is it? – seems to think I'm a cold-blooded killer. Personally, I had the impression that he has a chip on his shoulder. I don't mind. After all, there is nothing they can do to an innocent man, is there?"

Amy gave a non-committal nod, wishing she had been there during the interview and seen McCord squaring up to Mrs Campbell.

"Andrew, this is a murder inquiry," John reminded his brother. "They'll be digging up anything anybody has been up to in their past. What is there to find?"

Andrew shrugged again.

"You know, the usual. A bit of cannabis and coke at uni, a bit of gambling among friends, no harm done. Do you think the papers would make a big story out of it? Country Estate Heir's Depraved Youth Exposed?"

"This is not funny, Andrew," John snapped. "It is not only your reputation that is at stake here but also Mama's and mine. And Father's, for that matter. Have you ever given that a moment's thought? Of course, you haven't."

"I think you're making a mountain out of a molehill, dear brother. Relax. A little sherry?" he asked Amy, pointing to the decanter on the sideboard.

She shook her head.

"A little too early for me, I'm afraid."

"And you are driving, John, so as the upstanding citizen that you are, you can't have one," Andrew said with a smirk.

He opened the drinks cabinet and poured himself a careful measure of a twenty-year-old Laphroaig.

"What about your alibi?" John persisted. "If you have a watertight alibi, I suppose the police will stop digging. Where were you yesterday morning at half seven?"

Andrew laughed.

"What a silly question. In bed, of course."

"Mama saw you at around ten but in theory, you could have got up earlier, driven to Dunsapie Loch and been back for half nine. Plenty of time to kill Robbie and be back pretending to have been in bed all along."

While listening to his brother, Andrew's nonchalance had disappeared.

"Now listen here, John, what is this? Are you the prosecuting attorney now? Are you trying to drop me in it and have me arrested on suspicion of murder so you can get your hands on the whole estate?"

John ignored this remark.

"I am just thinking the way the police will think. Nobody actually saw you during the time of the murder, and Mama is not exactly the most credible witness where you are concerned."

Andrew and John both looked gloomy.

"You have forgotten an important point, though," Amy said. "There is no motive. No motive, no problem."

Andrew brightened up.

"This girl is not only stunningly beautiful; she is also more intelligent than either of us." Andrew beamed. "I had no reason in the big wide world to kill Robbie. He was an old friend." He paused briefly. "Possibly my oldest friend, come to think of it."

This realisation briefly seemed to dampen Andrew's spirits, but not for long.

"Stop fretting, dear brother," he said brightly, "everything will be fine."

He looked at his watch and bounced out of his chair. "Look at the time. I must be off. I'm meeting a lady for lunch who is not accustomed to waiting. Thank you for coming and calming down Mama, but I don't think you need to trouble yourselves any further."

John and Amy accompanied him through the hall, waving to Edith Campbell, still engrossed in her telephone conversation with Lady Smythe-Tennyson.

They stepped out into the chill autumn wind and watched Andrew squeeze himself into his cabriolet.

"You should not be driving," John reprimanded his brother.

Andrew shrugged off the censure in his brother's voice.

"I just seem to soak it up." He laughed and banged the door shut. "Goodbye, all. Wish me luck!"

And with that he was off.

"Are we going back then?" Amy asked, frustrated at the fruitless outing.

"First, I would like to speak to the estate manager," John said and walked towards the estate office, which was tucked away in a recess on the east side of the building. Before they had reached the door, they were confronted with the broad frame of Justin Torrence who stood there watching their approach.

Amy was used to attracting men's attention but she found the gaze from his slate-grey eyes inquisitive rather than lecherous.

"Good morning, sir, miss," he greeted the pair of them politely. "Has anything happened? I saw the police were here yesterday, and now you are paying us a visit, too. Not bad news, I hope?"

John inclined his head.

"Well, sadly, one of the men who was here at the weekend has been murdered. His name was Robert McArthur, but the others called him Robbie. Did you happen to speak to him at all?"

Torrence shook his red mane regretfully.

"I just helped with the shoot and the lunch and didn't speak to any of them at all."

Or rather, they didn't speak to you, Amy corrected the statement in her head.

"Did you notice anything about the group? Anything that might explain what happened?" she asked.

"Not unless he was shot," Torrence said with a deadpan expression.

"What do you mean?" Amy asked, hopefully.

"Mr McArthur was a danger to the public and himself when he was holding a gun, and the others were not much better." He did not manage to conceal his contempt. "At one point I even wondered if the beaters were waving their white flags to surrender rather than flush out the grouse. Mr Campbell was the only one to shoot a couple of birds; he is a good marksman. How was Mr McArthur killed?"

"He was hit over the head with a rock," John said, knowing that this fact had been in the daily newspapers and was by now common knowledge anyway.

Torrence shook his head again and regretfully scratched his beard, which covered most of his face apart from the pale lips often seen in red-haired people.

"Terrible."

"Did they seem to get on well?" Amy persisted. She had the distinct feeling that this man had his eyes and ears everywhere on the estate. "What were they talking about?"

"Mr McArthur tried to persuade Mr Buchan to get fitter and suggested jogging with him round Arthur's Seat in the morning at sunrise."

Torrence hesitated just long enough for John and Amy to understand that there was something else. "I wouldn't want to get anybody into trouble. You know, loose lips…" His voice trailed off.

"Please, Justin, tell us what you know," John urged him. "It might well help my brother."

"The police don't suspect him, do they?" Justin asked.

"No, absolutely not," John assured him. "What is it you wanted to say?"

"There was some argument between Mr McArthur and the other gentleman called Zacharias Walker. It had something to do with money, I'm not sure what exactly, but Mr McArthur was very angry, and then there was a bit of an atmosphere. I didn't see them afterwards, I just noticed them leaving late morning on Sunday."

"Thank you, Justin, you're a good man. I don't know what my mother would do without you," John said.

"Your mother and your brother have been very good to *me*," the estate manager replied. "They gave me this job when I was in dire straits, and I like it here."

"That is great to hear," John said. "Take care and look after this place for me, will you?"

Torrence nodded and briefly touching his cap returned to his office.

"So, your little brother has not been straight with us," Amy stated, anger in her voice. "He didn't say anything about an argument. Does he not realize how serious this is? A man has been murdered!"

"That is just typical of Andrew," John said. "Life is just a game to him."

Amy shook her head. "With an adversary like McCord, he needs to be careful not to overplay his hand."

They gazed into the distance where a fast-moving red dot was still visible on the thin grey line winding its way towards the city. John sighed.

"As soon as he has finished his date, I shall get hold of him and ask him about Zacharias Walker and what he and Robbie McArthur were arguing about."

Chapter 6

Duncan Calderwood dropped a couple of files on McCord's desk.

"The PM report and preliminary forensics," he announced.

"Anything new?" McCord asked, desperate for a breakthrough.

"Not really. The rock found at the scene has been confirmed as the murder weapon, but it's not a type that is commonly found in the vicinity of Arthur's Seat. They're looking into it. No news yet on the cigarette stub; I don't know why the DNA analysis is taking so long."

"Great," McCord grunted. "We'll come across as real super sleuths when Miss Thornton arrives."

"Oh?" Calderwood raised his eyebrows. "Has she got something for us?"

"So she says," McCord said sceptically. "Usually, it is a wild theory that will be superseded by a different one the next day."

"At least I *have* a theory," a voice resonated from the corridor, closely followed by the slim, elegant figure of Amy Thornton. She stood in the door frame for a second, clearly enjoying McCord's discomfort and wondering if the glow on his face originated from the overheated room or his embarrassment.

"Stop eavesdropping and tell us what you've got," McCord said gruffly.

Amy entered the room and sat down on the chair in front of McCord's desk.

"Can I get you a coffee?" DC Calderwood asked solicitously.

Amy gave him one of her irresistible smiles.

"No, thank you, I'm fine. I would never touch the brew from that machine. In fact, you should speak to your union representative about that. I'm sure having to drink that stuff can be classed as physical abuse."

Calderwood laughed and was about to reply when McCord butted in.

"Enough of the chit-chat. Do you have something pertinent to this inquiry or not?"

Amy put on a serious face.

"I have. John and I have spoken to the estate manager, and he told us that during the shoot on Saturday there was an argument between a Zacharias Walker and the murder victim. He was not sure of the detail, but it was definitely about money. Apparently, Robbie McArthur was very angry."

"Just a pity that Robbie McArthur has been murdered, and not Zacharias Walker. Usually, it is the angry one who does the killing, not the other way round."

"Don't be facetious," Amy retorted. "McArthur could have threatened Walker with something, and he decided to shut him up. What kind of guy is this Zacharias Walker anyway?"

"He's an investment broker," Calderwood replied eagerly. "Maybe we should look a little deeper into his financial affairs."

"You definitely should," Amy said approvingly, as if glad that at least someone involved in the inquiry was on the ball. "The estate manager also said that Robbie told them all that he went jogging round Arthur's Seat every morning at dawn. That means Walker could have known where and when to lie in wait for him, don't you think, DC Calderwood?" she asked, ignoring McCord.

"So could Andrew Campbell and the other guy," McCord said, asserting his presence and, for what it was worth, authority.

"You have nothing on Andrew," Amy pointed out. "He was in bed when Robbie was murdered, and anyway, he's not the type."

McCord shook his head.

"Get real. Just because he is upper-class and John's brother, he can't be a murderer? Everyone can be a murderer given the right, or rather, wrong, circumstances."

"Do you really believe that?" Amy asked, with a sudden involuntary shiver.

"I do," McCord said. "If I lined up a group of people with a murderer in it, I bet you would not be able to pick him out."

"Maybe not," Amy said, sounding unconvinced.

"And Andrew lied to you about the argument, didn't he?" McCord challenged her.

"He didn't exactly lie," Amy said, defending Andrew. "He just failed to mention it." Realizing how weak that sounded, she quickly moved on. "John asked him about the conversation, and he said it was just about an investment, and Robbie was probably jealous of all the money Walker makes on the stock market. That could very well be true, but I would look into it anyway if I were you."

"Thank you for the advice," McCord said sarcastically.

"You're welcome," Amy answered with a majestic wave of her hand. "Is there anything at all you have found out while I have been busy investigating your case?"

"You are supposed to assist us with our investigation, not the other way round," McCord reminded her. "However, since you are closely connected to Campbell family, your insights could prove valuable to us."

"How generous of you," Amy retorted, now in a sarcastic tone herself. "So, in return for what I find out, you're going to tell me what you haven't found out? Is that the deal?"

"The deal is that you will treat all information we give you as confidential and only use it to further our investigation," McCord explained.

"I would never do anything else," Amy said quietly, looking hurt.

"There might be situations that are difficult for you because your family is involved," McCord said. "You must be prepared to accept an outcome that you don't like."

"I like finding out the truth and bringing bad guys to justice, regardless. You know that from the last time we worked together," she told McCord.

"True," he conceded.

Amy raised her perfectly plucked eyebrows.

"Now that this is all settled, do you have anything at all for me?"

"We do," Calderwood blurted out before McCord had a chance to speak. "When they were at university, Alex Buchan, the other guy on the shoot, was in love with a girl that McArthur was going out with. He assaulted McArthur in public, accusing him of mistreating her. It's all in the files, but no charges were brought, and Buchan claims they kissed and made up afterwards."

Amy had perked up in her seat and taken out her notebook.

"What was the girl's name?"

"Cheryl Langley."

She jotted it down and got up. "I'll see what I can find out about her. Thanks, DC Calderwood, see you soon."

"I look forward to that," Calderwood stammered and saw her to the door, while McCord stayed at his desk, quietly fuming.

* * *

McCord approached DC Sutton's desk with due caution until he had entered her limited peripheral vision and waited for her to turn her long, bespectacled face and hugely enlarged eyes towards him. A brief nod told him it was acceptable to enter her space.

"Anything on Zacharias Walker, DC Sutton?" he asked. "DC Calderwood and I are going to interview him later this evening, and it would be good to have some ammunition."

He knew instantly this was a mistake as DC Sutton's brain would process the possibility of an armed assault on Walker that she was supposed to facilitate.

"Not literally," McCord added hastily, "I mean it would be good to have some background on him, especially things he might not want us to know."

DC Sutton nodded irritably. "Makes a lot of money in shares. Often sells just before a big slump and buys just before a big rise. Too much of a coincidence."

"Insider dealing?" McCord asked.

She avoided his gaze. "No proof yet."

"Thank you, DC Sutton, well done. Keep digging... I mean, keep looking."

Returning to his office, he was irritated to find Calderwood still hunched over his computer rather than being ready to grill Zacharias Walker, but his colleague greeted him with a triumphant look.

"Something was niggling at my brain," Calderwood said. "I don't know how we could have missed it."

"What *are* you on about?" McCord asked irritably. There were enough unanswered questions slushing through his brain without Calderwood talking in riddles.

"Edinburgh University. They all went to Edinburgh University together."

"We already knew that," said McCord, wondering if he had overworked the young man.

"But we didn't think of Jordan Lamond, the murder victim from The Shamrock. He was also at Edinburgh Uni, and not only that; he was in the same year as Robert McArthur, Andrew Campbell, Alexander Buchan and Zacharias Walker. There is even a photo of the five of them in the uni yearbook. 'The Players', they called themselves."

"Well now," McCord said, barely suppressing his excitement. "That *is* quite a coincidence. Do we believe in such coincidences?"

Calderwood shook his head, beaming with pride at his first breakthrough. McCord smiled, but it was the mirthless grin of the hunter who has spotted his prey.

"Let's go then and ask this Mr Walker about his university chums."

* * *

Zacharias Walker resided in Eglinton Crescent, not far from the German embassy, in the high-ceilinged flat above his stockbroker's business. His overly friendly demeanour told McCord that they had been expected and that the man was prepared.

"Please have a seat. Can I get you a drink, gentlemen?" he asked, pointing to the minibar in the corner of the living room. "Tea? Coffee?"

The detectives politely declined. A faint smell of pepperoni was lingering in the flat, and McCord realized that he was starving. He looked around and spotted an open pizza carton on the floor in the adjoining room, which he assumed was the study. Zacharias Walker followed his gaze.

"I often work from home in the evening, and then I just order a take-away. Bad habit," he added, pointing to his expanding waistline. "Now, what would you like to know?"

"Could you tell us about last weekend? Did you notice anything unusual about Robbie McArthur?"

"Nothing at all," Walker answered, a little too quickly. "We had a lovely weekend shooting, playing cards and having dinner together."

McCord pointedly looked at Calderwood, who nodded. The same phrases Buchan had used, well-rehearsed by the sound of it.

"Do you have an alibi for Monday morning around seven thirty?" McCord asked suddenly.

The investment banker almost jumped out of his seat.

"An alibi? What do you mean?"

"It means we would like to know where you were when Robert McArthur was murdered," McCord explained, intentionally misunderstanding the question.

Walker scowled.

"I was here, having my breakfast."

"Any witnesses?" McCord enquired.

"No, there were no witnesses," Walker snapped. "As you can see, I live alone. Surely you don't suspect *me*? Robbie and I were old friends!"

McCord shrugged.

"Old friends can bear old grudges. Or new ones," he added. "Did you not propose an investment to your friends that caused a bit of a falling out?"

Walker's eyes darted from one detective to the other. He laughed unconvincingly.

"Just a little misunderstanding. Robbie was offended that I suggested an investment that carried a higher risk for a higher yield. Ever since he got married and had a child, Robbie had become rather risk averse. Understandable if you are responsible for a family, and not just yourself."

"Completely understandable," McCord agreed, unconvincingly, and there was an uncomfortable pause until McCord added, "You wouldn't mind giving us a DNA sample, would you?"

"What? Eh, no, of course not," Walker hastily agreed, clearly discomfited. "But I swear, I had nothing to do with Robbie's death. Maybe you should ask Alex, Alex Buchan."

"Ah?" McCord leaned forward. "What should we be asking Mr Buchan about?"

"Well, when we were at uni together, Alex and Robbie fancied the same girl."

McCord hesitated, momentarily unable to remember her name.

"Cheryl, was it?" Calderwood came to the rescue, and Walker seemed gratified that the police knew about this matter.

"You are well informed," he said. "So, you know about the assault as well?"

McCord nodded. "We do. Mr McArthur did not press charges, though. If I were Mr Buchan, I'd be grateful for that. Why would Mr Buchan still hold a grudge after all these years?"

"I don't know." Walker attempted a retreat, but McCord was not going to let this go.

"What exactly did Mr McArthur do to the girl that upset Mr Buchan so much?"

"Oh, did he not tell you?" Walker asked with feigned surprise. "Robbie got her pregnant but did not want to commit to a serious relationship. Alex was furious. He really loved her, but she just wasn't interested."

"So that's how it was," McCord said.

"Not that I would believe for a minute that Alex could do anything like that, I mean, murder, that just doesn't happen…"

"In our circles?" McCord finished the sentence. "I'm surprised to hear you say that. What about Jordan Lamond?"

Walker looked completely confused. "What about him?"

"Does it not strike you as odd that two of your university friends have been murdered?"

"No… yes," Walker stammered, "of course, but Jordan's death had nothing to do with us at all…"

"So Mr McArthur's did?" McCord pressed home his advantage.

"I didn't say that!" Walker's voice became shrill. "Don't put words in my mouth. Poor Jordan died months ago. Was it not an accident?"

"We don't think so," McCord said coolly. "What was your relationship with Mr Lamond?"

"There hardly was one." Walker's voice had taken on a pleading note. "He was a bit of a loser, to be honest; went abroad, tried this and that and ended up working for his dad. He would join us for dinner when we all met in Edinburgh, but we didn't have that much in common anymore."

At least not status or money, McCord thought. Walker made him think of a fat dung beetle that he would like to squash under his foot.

"DC Calderwood will take your DNA sample now."

Calderwood put his notebook away and took a small cardboard box out of his coat pocket.

"Open your mouth, please," Calderwood said cheerfully, waving a cotton swab in front of Walker's face. "It won't take a second."

Walker swallowed and reluctantly parted his lips.

Calderwood rubbed the cotton bud along the inside of Walker's cheek, pulled it out, placed it carefully into a long, clear plastic tube and labelled it with name and date. "Thank you."

Walker swallowed again.

"I think that is enough for today, Mr Walker," McCord said. "Please don't leave town without telling us."

* * *

"I can't see the motive for Buchan to kill McArthur," McCord said when they climbed back into his Juke. "He is married, so why kill him over an old affair after all this time?"

Calderwood leaned back in his seat. "Buchan's marriage doesn't seem to be made in heaven, though. His wife had no idea about Cheryl. Maybe he married her for money and still carries a torch for Cheryl?"

"Maybe. Something must have triggered it, though. We need to talk to this Cheryl and see what her story is. But first thing tomorrow morning we are going to pay Mr Campbell another visit and ask him why he hasn't been straight with us."

Chapter 7

"Is it official police procedure to drag witnesses out of bed on a daily basis? You *are* aware that sleep deprivation is classified as a form of torture? There is also an amazing invention called a telephone that you could make use of and save taxpayers' money. But then you probably enjoy a jaunt into the countryside?"

Andrew Campbell's light-hearted tone had an edge to it this morning. He had dark shadows under his eyes, and his usual flamboyance had lost some of its sparkle.

"I prefer face-to-face conversations," McCord replied, not rising to the bait. "They tell you a lot more than words."

"And which dark secrets have you unearthed by seeing me in person this morning? Lucy!" he shouted into the hall. "Where is the bloody coffee?"

"For example," McCord continued, ignoring the outburst, "I know now that you have not slept well. A guilty conscience? Because you didn't tell us the truth last time we were here?"

Andrew Campbell feigned shock. "Are you accusing me of lying?"

"You didn't tell us about the investment offer that Mr Walker made you all, causing an argument between Mr McArthur and Mr Walker, and you didn't tell us about the history between Mr Buchan and Mr McArthur either. Care to elaborate on these points now? I would hate to come back tomorrow morning with more follow-up questions."

Andrew Campbell's jocular demeanour had given way to a steely coldness. He was very much his mother's son, McCord thought, but without her self-discipline.

"Firstly, I did not *lie*. If I didn't tell you everything that went on it was because I felt it had no bearing on the case and, secondly, I'm not a snitch."

McCord leaned forward and lowered his voice making it sound more threatening than any shouting would have done.

"*I* decide what has or has not any bearing on this case, is that clear?"

Then he leaned back, seeming suddenly relaxed and cheerful.

"Doesn't it worry you at all that two of your university friends have been murdered within months?"

Andrew Campbell looked puzzled.

"Two?"

"Jordan Lamond in March, and now Robbie McArthur. You see, my problem is that you don't seem shocked at all, which makes me think that you might be involved..."

"Now listen here," Campbell raised his voice, only to be silenced by an imperious gesture of McCord's hand.

"...and you also don't seem to be worried for your own safety, which leads me to the same conclusion. So, if you *are* indeed innocent, Mr Campbell, I would advise you to start worrying and cooperating fully. Currently, there is a DNA test being carried out on a cigarette stub found at the murder scene. Which brand is it that you smoke?"

"Marlboro," Campbell said, dismissively.

McCord exchanged a glance with Calderwood.

"Is there anything you want to tell me now before the results come in?" McCord asked.

"Nothing at all, and next time you want to speak to me, make an appointment so that I can have my solicitor present."

"That is perfectly within your rights," McCord said. "And we are perfectly within our rights to take a DNA sample from you. I'm sure you are keen to be eliminated from our enquiries as soon as possible."

Calderwood held up the cotton bud. "Open wide," he said.

Andrew Campbell looked furious but obeyed. After the sample had been labelled and stored away, he rose, indicating that the meeting was over.

"It was a pleasure." McCord smiled insincerely without bothering to get up. "But before I go, I'd like a word with your housekeeper, Lucy, and your estate manager. Meanwhile, think carefully about what I've said."

Right on cue, Lucy appeared with the heavy tray in the doorway.

"Put the coffee down on the table," Campbell told her, "and then the inspector wants to ask you a few questions." He poured himself a cup of coffee and grabbed a couple of biscuits from the plate. "Goodbye, Inspector. Good luck with your investigation."

Executing an ironic bow, he left the room, while the anxious-looking housekeeper was standing forlorn in front of the detectives. McCord signalled to Calderwood to do the questioning since Lucy seemed less intimidated by the young, good-looking DC.

Calderwood gave the faintest nod to show that he understood.

"No need to worry at all," Calderwood reassured Lucy. "Do you think we could all have a coffee?"

"Of course." Lucy leaned over the table to serve the coffee.

McCord, remembering what Edith Campbell had said about her, wondered why an attractive girl like her would dress in combat trousers and a baggy jumper that made her look rather frumpy. But then, he thought, she would be busy cleaning and cooking all day.

"I really have nothing to do with this whole business," Lucy declared after she had sat down, her legs tightly closed.

"Nobody is suspecting you of anything," Calderwood said. "We're just building up a picture, you know, background that helps us with our investigation."

Lucy took a sip of coffee, and then quickly picked up one of the posh biscuits.

McCord guessed that they were normally reserved for members of the family and guests.

She took a large bite of her ginger nut. "What would you like to know?"

"How long have you been working here?" Calderwood asked.

She waited for the biscuit to melt in her mouth before she answered.

"Seven months."

"Were you here on Monday morning?"

"Yes, from half eight until lunch time. I was busy tidying up after the weekend. It is only a part-time job, you know."

McCord exchanged a look with Calderwood. If Lucy had come as late as she claimed, she would not be able to confirm if Andrew Campbell had been at home during the time of the murder.

"You weren't here to help with the guests?"

"On the Friday, I got their rooms ready and prepared dinner, but I was gone by the time they arrived. Mrs Campbell asked if I could come in again on the Saturday and Sunday, but it was my friend's wedding down in England so I couldn't. Mrs Campbell was not best pleased."

"Had you met Mr Campbell's friends before by any chance?" Calderwood asked. "Robert McArthur, Alexander Buchan and Zacharias Walker; they call him Zac, I believe."

"Once," Lucy said evenly. "They spent a weekend up here in the spring."

"Did they get on well then?"

Lucy thought about that for a moment.

"They seemed to. They played poker and got drunk, you know what it's like."

"I imagine it is not easy working for the Campbells?" Calderwood winked conspiratorially.

Lucy chose her words carefully.

"They're okay, I guess."

"What do you think of Mr Campbell?" Calderwood asked casually.

She took another gulp of coffee before she answered.

"He was grumpy this morning, but that was because of you." She gave a smile that was difficult to interpret.

"He doesn't like to be bothered with anything before lunchtime. Or afterwards for that matter."

"So, who does all the work around here?" Calderwood wondered.

"Justin Torrence, the estate manager. That's his title, but they're paying him no better than a labourer." She lowered her voice to a whisper. "I don't know how he puts up with it all day, every day. He has the patience of a saint." Her eyes had a dreamy look but then she caught herself and put the last bit of the biscuit in her mouth.

She picked some crumbs off her jeans, careful not to drop any onto the carpet.

Calderwood glanced at his boss, who nodded slightly. There was nothing more to be gained from the housekeeper.

"Thank you very much, Lucy." Calderwood shook her hand, smiling. "We're going to have a word with Justin Torrence now if possible. Is he around?"

Lucy pulled out her phone to look at the time.

"He'll be having his morning break in his office. Sometimes, when Mrs Campbell is out, I go over and give him some of the leftovers from the kitchen. Come with me, I'll show you the way to the office."

With a mischievous grin, she sneaked a couple of foil-wrapped biscuits into her pockets and led the way.

* * *

When Lucy appeared in his office and introduced McCord and Calderwood, the estate manager did not seem surprised.

"I saw you arriving," he said by way of an explanation. "Did you find Mr Campbell?"

"We caught up with him, thank you," McCord said, "but it is you I wanted a word with."

Smiling at her colleague, Lucy put the biscuits on the desk, waved the men goodbye and left to get on with her chores.

"Aha?" Torrence raised his eyebrows. "Please sit down. How can I help you?"

"You told Mr John Campbell that you overheard a dispute between Mr McArthur and Mr Walker during the shoot on Saturday. Could you tell us more about that?"

Torrence shook his head.

"Just what I told Mr Campbell and the young lady who was here. It had to do with an investment, I'm not sure what exactly, and Mr McArthur got very angry with Mr Walker. The boss tried to calm him down, and then they just carried on with the shoot."

McCord tried not to show his disappointment. "Were you up and about early on Monday morning?"

"I'm up early every morning," Torrence said.

McCord could not detect any resentment in his voice. "Did you happen to see Mr Campbell about?"

"He is rarely up before ten o'clock. On Monday morning, he signed some paperwork and then went into town."

"Could he have gone out early and come back without you noticing?" McCord asked.

A tiny twitch around his mouth indicated that Torrence fully understood the implication of the question.

"His car was here, and I would have noticed a taxi arriving."

Calderwood snapped his notebook shut in frustration.

"Thank you very much for your time, Mr Torrence."

McCord made to leave but before he opened the door, he turned round.

"What's it like to work for the Campbells?"

The estate manager smiled. "The job suits me fine."

"I'm glad to hear that," McCord lied. "Take care now."

Chapter 8

It had not taken Amy long to find Cheryl Gibbs, née Langley, on social media. She was a prolific poster of photographs and not particularly careful about her privacy settings. Whatever had happened at university, it did not seem to have destroyed her life. There were lots of happy photographs with her husband William and friends. Amy had noticed, however, that there were no pictures of children.

Turning into Commercial Street at ten thirty, Amy immediately recognised the ghastly tangerine exterior of the vegan café she had spotted in the background of one of Cheryl's Facebook posts showing off her marital home. There had been no pictures relating to a job or work colleagues, so Amy had timed her arrival hoping to find Cheryl in and her husband out. She knew her chances of an interview were slim but there was no harm in trying.

Cheryl Gibbs and her husband lived on the top floor of a recently built block of flats overlooking Victoria Dock. Amy pressed the buzzer three times before the intercom crackled into action.

"Yes?" a tired female voice answered.

"Sorry to disturb you," Amy apologised. "Amy Thornton here from the magazine *Forth Write*. I was wondering if I could have a word."

"Definitely not," the voice at the other end snapped.

Amy waited for a moment to let curiosity kick in, and it did.

"What is this about?" the voice asked, slightly more friendly now.

"I'm making enquiries about the death of Mr Robert McArthur–"

"I don't know anything about that," the voice interrupted Amy nervously. "Please go away."

"Of course, I don't want to pester you," Amy said politely. "It's just that the police are investigating Mr McArthur's past, and your name has come up. They will no doubt want to speak to you."

There was an anxious pause.

"When I talked to them, I had the impression that they were more interested in your husband but–"

"Oh my God." There was panic in the voice now.

"Maybe I can help?" Amy suggested. "I'm working closely with the police on this case. Personally, I think they're clutching at straws. It might be better to discuss this in private, don't you think?"

There was another pause. Amy held her breath. After what seemed an age, the intercom hummed. Amy exhaled slowly. She pushed the door open and took the lift to the top floor.

* * *

The woman expecting her at the entrance to flat number ten bore no resemblance to the pretty, smiling Cheryl Gibbs on the Facebook page. Amy looked closely, and eventually recognised the cute baby face although now it was bloated and made Mrs Gibbs look like a slightly creepy doll. Her fashionable outfits had been replaced by baggy sweatpants and a loose-fitting T-shirt that did not manage to conceal the bulges underneath. She had not applied any make-up to conceal the unhealthy pallor of her skin, and above the shadows caused by sleepless nights, a pair of droopy eyes stared at Amy's radiant, olive skin and her elegant trouser suit with a mixture of envy and suspicion.

"Thank you for seeing me," Amy said, afraid to fall at this last hurdle, and determinedly walked past Mrs Gibbs into the flat. It was furnished with the cool, simple elegance that requires meticulous tidiness and does not go well with the neglect that this one had suffered. Peering into the living room, Amy noticed empty mugs that cluttered up the expensive wooden surfaces and the light grey carpet which had not been vacuumed for a while.

"Come in here." Mrs Gibbs commanded, rather than invited, Amy into the kitchen. On the table, there was an open letter from a clinic whose logo Amy recognised, but she pretended not to have seen it. Mrs Gibbs snatched it away and pointed to one of the ergonomically shaped chairs.

"Have a seat. Coffee? Tea?"

"Coffee, thanks."

For Mrs Gibbs, every interaction was clearly an effort. Amy decided to abandon the pretence and attempt a shot in the dark.

"I'm sorry you're not well. I have a friend who went through fertility treatment, and she said it was hellish."

Taken by surprise and, at the same time, moved by the sympathy in Amy's voice, Mrs Gibbs' defences crumbled.

"It is awful," she admitted, close to tears, "and it goes on and on and never seems to lead to anything. But it simply must. Will and I have always wanted children."

"It's not the first round then?" Amy asked.

"The third. Not counting the three attempts by the NHS. They eventually told us there is no more they can do, so we had to go private."

Amy tried to imagine the strain, financially and emotionally, but could not. "I'm very sorry," she repeated. "I really hope it works out for you this time."

"Thanks. God, I forgot all about the coffee. These hormones turn your brain to mush. Half the time I don't know if I'm coming or going."

Mrs Gibbs unscrewed the lid of the instant coffee jar, and Amy half hoped she would forget about the coffee altogether.

"You don't need to worry about the police" – Amy tried to come back to the purpose of her visit – "as long as you're straight with them. They're not out to get you or your husband. At the moment, they're just filling in the background, to get the bigger picture as it were. Your name came up in connection with Robbie McArthur, and I just wondered what went on between the two of you."

The spoon, heaped with mud-coloured granules, stopped halfway to the fashionably wonky mug.

"We were an item at uni," Mrs Gibbs said in a flat voice, keeping her face turned away. "Ancient history." She managed to get the coffee into the two mugs and lifted the kettle.

Amy did not like the idea of two pints of boiling water in the hands of an unstable woman but pressed on, nonetheless.

"The police have a record of an assault by Alexander Buchan on Robbie, during which he accused Robbie of having behaved very badly towards you. What was that all about?"

Mrs Gibbs doggedly continued with her task as if it required all her concentration. She spilled some of the water onto the marble worktop but made no attempt to wipe it off.

"I suppose it's common knowledge anyway. I fell pregnant and Robbie got cold feet. Alex was in love with me, I guess, and he was angry with Robbie, that was all. They made up afterwards. I really don't know why these old stories are being dragged up now."

"The police have to look at everything, that is their job," Amy reassured her. "What happened to the baby?"

Mrs Gibbs put down the kettle in a slow, deliberate motion.

"I was lucky, I had a miscarriage a couple of weeks afterwards anyway. Problem solved." She gave a bitter laugh.

The sound of the key in the door made her jump.

"Hi, sweetie," a deep voice shouted from the hall, "I've just come back to pick up some stuff for the office."

A tall man in a sharp suit appeared in the kitchen door. Seeing Amy half rising from her chair, he stopped in his move to embrace his wife.

"Who are you?" he asked suspiciously.

"I'm Amy Thornton, nice to meet you."

She thought it better not to reveal her job or the true purpose of her visit. William Gibbs turned to his wife.

"You never mentioned an Amy before? How do you know each other?"

Amy could not decide whether his demeanour was threatening or not, but Mrs Gibbs was paralysed. Not getting an answer from his wife, Gibbs looked at Amy for the answer.

"I... I visited your wife today to tell her that the police are interested in her because her name came up during the investigation into Robert McArthur's murder."

His eyes narrowed.

"But you are not with the police?"

Amy saw no way of wriggling out of this.

"No, I work for the magazine *Forth Write*," she admitted.

"A journalist?" He almost choked on the word, then turned to his wife, his suspicion turning into anger. "You've been blabbing to a *journalist*?"

"She hasn't told me anything," Amy hastily intervened. "I just wanted to give her the opportunity to tell her side of the story."

He swivelled around to face Amy.

"There is no story, and now get out and don't show your face here ever again!"

Amy thought it best not to argue and made a hasty retreat with as much dignity as she could muster. After the door had slammed shut behind her, she hung about on the upper floor for a while, trying to hear what was going on inside. She sincerely hoped that Gibbs would not vent his anger on his wife, but she could not hear a thing. She decided to get out before he found her loitering on the doorstep and pressed the down button of the lift.

* * *

Desperate for a decent coffee and a Danish pastry, Amy gave the tangerine vegan café a miss and walked down a side street where a wooden signboard on the pavement advertised exactly what she was looking for. A few minutes later, chewing thoughtfully on a cinnamon swirl, she reran the last half hour in her head. Of course, many people resented the press for the intrusion into their privacy, but Gibbs had used the word 'blabbing'. 'Blabbing' implied that they, or one of them, had something to hide. But what? Mrs Gibbs had said herself that her relationship with Robbie and the pregnancy was common knowledge at the time.

The irony of it – to become pregnant by mistake, and then… Amy dropped the rest of her cinnamon swirl and licked her sticky fingers in a very unladylike manner. What if the irony was even more bitter than Mrs Gibbs had admitted? What if she had not lost the baby but had had an abortion? Abandoned by the father of the child, she would have been worried about destroying her own future. If she had no support from her parents, she might not have seen any other way out. And what if – Amy took another sip of coffee to give her braincells that final push – what if that abortion had been botched and left her infertile? Reduced her to the sick, vulnerable woman she was now and put her marriage under unimaginable strain? How did Gibbs feel, knowing that after ruining his and his wife's happiness Robbie went on to enjoy a son with another woman? Maybe there had come a point where Gibbs had given up hope and decided to take revenge?

Amy pulled out her phone and called McCord, but there was no answer. Maybe just as well. So far, all she had was conjecture, and McCord hated conjecture. She would have to find proof.

* * *

After another latte and a sweep around social media platforms populated by anonymous users, Amy had a list of medical establishments who might not ask too many questions if a girl turned to them in her hour of need. Looking down her silky trousers, she decided that she needed a disguise. A charity shop nearby provided all she needed: a pair of faded, ill-fitting jeans, a cheap top and, horror of horrors, trainers. In the changing room, she loosened and messed up her carefully pinned-up hair and wiped off her make-up with a tissue. Looking at herself in the mirror, she realised for the first time that clothes really did make people.

She started with the most highly recommended address, which was only a short walk away. A sign in the window promised free advice and support for women with health issues, and true enough, once inside, Amy was greeted warmly by a young woman in tailored slacks and a white coat who was standing behind a desk, filing a form. Amy approached with the hesitancy and wariness she supposed were common in this situation and smiled shyly at the receptionist.

"Hi, I'm Cheryl Langley. I've been here before, and I was wondering if you could help me again."

"Sure," the woman beamed. "Please, come through."

She led Amy to a small consulting room and pointed to one of the chairs. She seemed to be a little more than just a receptionist. Maybe a nurse?

"What seems to be the problem?"

"Well," Amy mumbled, "I forgot to take the pill, and now I'm in big trouble."

The woman nodded sympathetically and sat down next to Amy.

"How long ago was it? The morning after pill might still work for you?"

"It's definitely too late for that," Amy said, "and there is no way…" She hid her face in a tissue, wiping her eyes.

"Have you been to your GP? Talked to your partner and your parents? Sometimes, after the first shock, things don't seem too bad," the nurse suggested.

Amy sniffed.

"My GP is an old family friend, and my parents are very religious. The man in question is married and just told me he is never going to leave his family. There is no way…"

Amy's voice took on a hysterical note as she ran out of ideas.

"It's fine, don't worry, we'll sort something out for you," the nurse said soothingly. "The doctor will check you over as soon as he is free. You said you were here before? Strange, I don't remember you, and normally I never forget a face."

"It was quite a while ago," Amy said, firmly deciding on a retreat before the gynaecological examination.

"Let me have a look at your file then, while you're waiting."

Relieved, Amy jumped up and followed the nurse into the still deserted reception area.

"Langley, Cheryl," the nurse repeated while typing the name into the computer. She waited for a few seconds, then shook her head, frowning.

"That's odd, we have no record of you. Are you sure this is the name you used at the time?"

"Positive," Amy said. "Actually, now that I'm here, I'm not so sure this is the best way to do things. Maybe you're right and I should talk to my parents. If they love me, they will love my baby too, won't they?"

The receptionist looked up, seemingly used to sudden change of hearts.

"It is true, after the first shock, many families come round and end up delighted with a new addition."

Amy was already at the door.

"Thank you so much for helping me see sense," she said, rushing out.

"Good luck!" the nurse called after her.

After four further futile attempts, some in rather unsavoury places, Amy decided to make her way home. Thank God she had not told McCord anything about this – she could imagine the look on his face and the cutting remark that would accompany it. She wished now that she had not wasted the whole afternoon on her suspicion of an abortion instead of doing some packing. There was less than a week left until she had to move out of the flat where she had spent her whole life. She was not sure how she felt about that. It was high time to get her own place, but with the extortionate rents and house prices in Edinburgh, it made sense to move into the flat that came with her mother's new shop, while Valerie moved in with John. Not quite independence yet, but at least she would have the place to herself.

Just then a shaft of evening sun squeezed past the darkening clouds and illuminated a brass plaque on the stone wall of the Georgian building she was passing. Having been brought up with the mysteries of the catholic doctrine, Amy had never quite shaken off her belief in divine signs. She rang the bell and pushed open the heavy wooden door.

The receptionist, a prim woman in her fifties, glanced at the clock promising closing time in five minutes and looked Amy up and down. Wrong outfit again. Amy thought of the creased mess her silk trousers had become in her bag, and maybe it was the genuine pain in her face that prompted the receptionist to listen to Amy's spiel, but when she mentioned Cheryl's name, a shadow moved across the stern face.

"Cheryl Langley?" she asked with narrowing eyes.

"That's right," Amy confirmed with a fluttering in her stomach.

"I don't think so." The woman stared at her face. "I know Cheryl Langley, or rather Gibbs, and you look nothing like her. Who are you, a journalist? The matter has been to court and settled. There is no story. I suggest you leave our premises immediately, or I'll call the police."

Amy did not need to be told twice. She heaved open the door and ran down the street towards St Leonard's. No story – aye right!

Chapter 9

St Leonard's resembled a busy anthill as the day shift was leaving and the nightshift arriving. Amy greeted everybody with a fleeting smile as she rushed towards McCord's office, but most people did not recognise her at first. Some of the staff regarded her easy access to the

DI as improper although nobody seriously believed that the unconventional arrangement did any harm; on the contrary, they had all benefitted from the positive coverage in *Forth Write* magazine as the Super's smile shone upon them all during those weeks. Some romantics even had a bet going on when DI McCord and the pretty journalist would finally get together. Needless to say, they kept the wager a secret from McCord, who, if he found out, would send them to the council rubbish dump next time it needed sifting for evidence.

McCord was still in his office, and so was Calderwood, both mightily frustrated at the lack of progress. The DC's eyes lit up as Amy breezed into the office.

"Miss Thornton!"

"Please call me Amy," she said, out of breath.

McCord did not like that they were on first name terms.

"I take it you have another theory, Miss Thornton?" he asked pointedly.

"Much more than that."

With a dramatic gesture she stuck a Post-it note on the only space on McCord's desk, which was otherwise littered with paperwork.

"What is this?" he asked warily, expecting either a ludicrous idea that would waste his time, or a new lead that she would gloat about. "And what *are* you wearing? Have you been working undercover in Niddrie without my knowledge?"

"Yes, and no," she said, looking over to Calderwood and gifting him with her most dazzling smile.

"This is the address of the clinic where Cheryl Gibbs, née Langley, had an abortion seven years ago. I believe they botched the operation and she sued them successfully. She and her husband are desperate to have children, so she is now on her sixth round of fertility treatment. If I were her husband, I'd have killed Robert McArthur many times over."

Calderwood looked impressed, but McCord had learned to be sceptical.

"And you know this how?" he asked.

Amy slumped onto the chair opposite McCord's desk and stretched out her legs. It was as if with the informal attire she had suddenly found a delicious freedom from her ingrained self-discipline.

McCord noticed this new persona with mixed feelings. He found her laddish demeanour both disturbing and sexy, and the fact that he was bothered by it, was the most unsettling aspect of all.

"I went to the Gibbs' flat," Amy told them. "Cheryl Gibbs is not well; the treatment has knocked her for six, and she is losing hope that it will ever work."

"She let you, a reporter she had never seen before, into the house and told you all about the abortion?" McCord asked incredulously. A terrible thought occurred to him. "You didn't tell her you were with the police, did you?"

"Not exactly," Amy said evasively.

"What do you mean 'not exactly'?" McCord's voice had risen to a level that drew colleagues into the corridor where they tried to look busy. He jumped out of his chair and slammed the door shut.

Amy exhaled loudly. "Why are you always so pedantic? Do I not get results in the end?"

"Not if you act illegally!" McCord's anger was mounting.

"I merely suggested to her that the police might be interested in her history with a recent murder victim and that she might be better off talking to a sympathetic woman than to a boorish police inspector," Amy said.

McCord shook his head in silent fury. Before he had time to formulate his response, however, Amy quickly carried on.

"She claims that she had a miscarriage at the time, but I don't believe her. Then her husband appeared unexpectedly. He was evasive and rather aggressive."

"You don't say." McCord's voice was dripping with sarcasm. "You wheedle your way into a vulnerable woman's home and poke about in their most private affairs. How cooperative do you think they will be when Calderwood and I turn up there tomorrow? You've really done it this time!"

"I think Amy has done very well," Calderwood said. "It sounds as if we have a solid motive here, which is more than can be said about our other suspects."

McCord swung his chair round and glared at his DC.

"And how did our clever Miss Thornton get the address of the clinic that – allegedly – performed the abortion? No, wait, let me guess... It was in a way that will make all gathered evidence inadmissible in court. Right, Miss Thornton?"

Amy tilted her head in a gesture of partial acquiescence.

"I pretended to be Cheryl Langley, but the woman told me all by herself that there had been a court case."

"And did she say what the court case was about?" McCord demanded. "I bet she didn't. Maybe Mrs Gibbs slipped outside their door on the ice in January and broke her ankle."

"Now you're just being silly," Amy said, clearly annoyed that her supreme efforts and skill were not being valued. "It all fits. All you have to do is to get a court order to see their patient records, and then go to Mr Gibbs and ask him for his alibi."

And to McCord's chagrin, that was exactly what he ended up doing.

* * *

When Amy finally made it back to the magazine, her colleague Martin Eden – subeditor responsible for politics and creator of popular cartoons – was all aflutter. With his improbably black, stencilled eyebrows, permanently puckered lips and garishly colourful outfits, Martin resembled an evil parrot but was, in fact, John's oldest friend and Amy's greatest fan.

In a dramatic whisper he told her that John was waiting for her.

Feeling guilty about spending all day on the murder hunt rather than her paid job, Amy rushed over to his office and gently knocked on the door.

John was flicking through some papers when he called her in.

"Are you remembering that we need to finalise the weekend edition today?" he asked, lifting his eyes and looking her up and down. "Where have you been? And why are you looking like – that?" He pointed vaguely to her scruffy appearance.

"I'm trying to solve a murder and get your brother's neck out of the noose," Amy retorted. "How is it that I run myself ragged and nobody appreciates it?"

"Of course, I appreciate what you do," John hastily assured her. "But the clock is ticking. Before I send it all off to the printer's, I wanted to make sure you agree for now that we keep quiet about the whole affair."

Amy frowned, not at all enamoured with the idea that there should be a weekend edition without mentioning the case everybody was talking about.

"We need to say *something* about the murder," she insisted. "All the other papers are full of it."

"We are not the other papers," John said, just as the phone rang. With an apologetic look towards Amy, he picked up the receiver.

"Good evening, Mama. How–"

A shrill tirade interrupted his pleasantries. John listened patiently, motioning Amy to wait.

"Yes, Mama… no, Mama, I am actually in a meeting, Mama, discussing the weekend edition. Yes… No… You have to understand, Mama... Of course, I shall do what I can, Mama. Goodbye."

With the worn-out look he always had after dealing with his mother, John put the receiver down.

"Let me guess," Amy said. "She wants us to run a thirty-page dossier on Saturday on the splendour of the Campbell family in general and Andrew's innocence in particular?"

"Something like that," John said, wearily. "But officially we do not know any more than anybody else, which is close to zero, and anything we say in favour of Andrew will be interpreted as bias."

"But if we don't say anything, it sounds as if we have no faith in him or even something to hide."

John sighed.

"Damned if we do and damned if we don't," he said.

Amy thought about it for a moment.

"Let's just stick to the facts, but I'll mention that, according to our sources, Andrew is not a suspect and that the police are looking at different lines of inquiry."

"I am not sure DI McCord would subscribe to that. From what Andrew and my mother are saying, he seems to have it in for him."

"But he hasn't arrested him, has he?" Amy said. "And what is going on in DI McCord's mind is anybody's guess."

John nodded. "Agreed. Go with that."

Chapter 10

"You– must– be– joking." McCord enunciated each word. He listened to the nervous explanation at the other end of the line, while drumming a gallop on the desk with his fingers. "Okay, okay," he interrupted the breathless voice, unable to stay on the phone any longer without swearing. "Just get it done."

He slammed the receiver down and met Duncan Calderwood's curious eyes.

"Some bloody fool has sent the DNA sample from the cigarette stub to the wrong lab. It'll be another forty-eight hours at least."

Calderwood shook his head. "Damn."

A cheerful 'good afternoon' echoed through the corridor outside, and Calderwood beamed as Amy Thornton knocked on the open door and entered the office without awaiting a further invitation.

Calderwood jumped up. "Amy, how nice to see you!"

"And you, Duncan. Any news on our prime suspect, DI McCord?"

McCord exhaled audibly.

"*My* prime suspect still prances around on his posh estate."

Amy pulled a face.

"You've checked Cheryl Gibbs' medical records and her husband's alibi?" she demanded.

"Indeed, I have," McCord said. "And many an hour I spent on this theory of yours."

"And?" Amy was unable to conceal her irritation. "You're not telling me I was wrong about the abortion?"

McCord shook his head reluctantly.

"Cheryl Langley, as she was then, did have an abortion that went wrong. After several failed attempts at getting pregnant again she was told that her problems were down to damage done during the procedure. She and her husband successfully sued the clinic and were awarded compensation, which they used to finance some of the private fertility treatments."

Amy sat up in her chair.

"So, plenty of motive. What about his alibi for Monday morning?"

"William Gibbs says he left early for a business trip to Manchester. He arrived there at lunchtime," Calderwood explained, obviously not content with being left out of the conversation.

"Time enough for a little detour past Dunsapie Loch, kill Robbie McArthur and get to Manchester in time for lunch," Amy said. "Have you checked his satnav?"

"I do know how to conduct a murder investigation, Miss Thornton," McCord growled. "Please, let me get on with my job. When we eventually get the DNA samples from the cigarette stub and from Andrew Campbell back, the case might be closed."

"But Andrew has an alibi!" Amy exclaimed. "Justin Torrence said he did not leave the estate that morning. And Andrew is not exactly a giant, either. To hit Robbie McArthur on the head, he would have had to stand on a stepladder. You are just wasting time and, on top of it, Mrs Campbell will accuse you of harassment. There is something we are missing!"

Calderwood nodded but wisely did not to aggravate his boss any further.

"Whether Andrew Campbell is innocent or not, I think we are right about the university connection," he said to McCord. "It seems too much of a coincidence that two members of a group are killed in a similar way within a few months."

"Two?" Amy asked. "Are you linking this to the murder in The Shamrock?"

"Yes," Calderwood said. "Lamond and McArthur were at university together, and I'll be looking again into the time they were there and see if anything comes up. Maybe you could help me with that, Amy?"

Before she had a chance to reply, McCord stood up.

"I'm sure Miss Thornton has packing to do. Are you not moving soon?"

Amy looked surprised that he had remembered. "Next week, but the sale of Mum's shop and flat is still not finalised. Apparently, the buyer is having second thoughts. And we only got the new premises because my mum promised them a quick sale. We can't delay now without losing the property. We might need a bridging loan unless the estate agent gets the buyer to sign on the dotted line soon. It's a nightmare!"

The men, who had both had their own experiences with the Edinburgh housing market, nodded sympathetically.

"If I can do anything," McCord offered, "like throwing the prospective buyer into a cell until he signs, just let me know."

Amy smiled.

"That won't be necessary but thank you. See you both soon."

"I hope it works out," Calderwood said to Amy's back.

McCord tried not to look pleased that it had sounded so lame.

* * *

On Saturday morning, Amy, her mother Valerie and John Campbell were waiting impatiently for the estate agent. He had told Valerie that the buyer wanted to have another look at the property on Monday and that they should think about sprucing the place up a bit. Valerie suspected that he had a hidden agenda to get her to drop the price and had summoned John and Amy as reinforcements. When the shop's doorbell rang, Amy discreetly mustered the round-faced, immaculately dressed man and took an instant, inexplicable dislike to him. She made an effort, however, and smiled politely as she shook his hand that exerted just the right amount of strength. You can rely on me, it said, but I won't force anything on you.

"Ms Thornton," he squealed in a high-pitched voice, turning to Valerie, "I am so sorry to bother you with this, *and* at the weekend, but I feel that we need a big push to get this sale through. Thank God the weather forecast is good; the place looks so much better in natural light."

His beady little pig's eyes darted around the room, clearly finding fault.

"Hmm."

Amy, who had helped her mother paint the shop only a few months ago, and John, who had bought the beautiful sofa for customers to sit on during consultations and the state-of-the-art coffee machine, exchanged a look of mutual understanding. They did not like this man.

"Would you like a coffee, Mr Buchan?" Valerie asked.

Amy felt her jaw drop.

"No, thank you; I have another appointment in half an hour," he squeaked.

Amy recovered quickly from the shock and moved surreptitiously closer to read the elegant ceramic name tag pinned to his lapel. Alexander Buchan. The guy who had thumped Robbie McArthur seven years ago for getting his flame pregnant and abandoning her. A potential killer or victim, but which? She tried to imagine him bashing Robbie McArthur's head in and came to the conclusion that it was possible. Then she pictured him lying on the floor in a pool of blood. Also possible. Maybe McCord was right, and everybody was a potential killer as well as a victim.

"Right," Alexander Buchan declared after pondering the situation. "The sofa has to go; it clutters up the room. If you could hang a mirror or two to create the illusion of spaciousness, that would be great. Move that monstrosity of a coffee machine next door as well but make some coffee just before my client is due – the smell creates a homely atmosphere. Polish the doorknobs and light switches; it has a disproportionate impact on how clean the room seems. Would you consider dropping the price?" he asked Valerie after a deliberate pause.

"No, we would not," John intervened, far too genteel to tell Mr Buchan who he thought the real knob in the room was.

"Splendid," Mr Buchan declared, despite clearly thinking the opposite. "Fingers crossed for Monday. Have a nice weekend."

He grabbed his damp coat which he had thrown carelessly over the delicate fabric of the sofa and opened the door.

"You too," Valerie managed to say before the doorbell jingled as he left. It sounded as if it was giggling.

As soon as Buchan had moved a few yards down the pavement, Amy pulled out her phone and scrolled through her contacts.

She silenced John and Valerie's questions with an impatient gesture of her hand as the connection was made.

"DI McCord? Sorry to bother you on a Saturday... That is true," she conceded when he pointed out that she had never had any qualms about bothering him at any time before. "Listen, you'll never guess who the estate agent selling my mum's shop is…" She waited for McCord to catch on. "It is. And I didn't like him one bit, even before I realised who he was." She listened for a moment, her face clouding over. "Well, if you have *that* attitude…" she grumbled. "Fine. Enjoy your weekend."

She hung up.

"What did he say?" Valerie asked.

Amy was in a huff.

"He said that a man is not necessarily a murderer just because I don't like him. The cheek! When he is doing exactly the same with Andrew."

She bit her tongue, but it was too late.

"DI McCord still suspects Andrew?" John exclaimed. "I thought the alibi would have sorted that out."

Amy shrugged.

"DI McCord has an inbred dislike of the upper class. He is fond of you, though, for some reason." She looked at him affectionately and smiled. "It must be the great coffee you make."

* * *

McCord put his phone away, annoyed with himself. Why was it that whenever he had any dealings with Amy Thornton, they ended up squabbling? She had an uncanny ability to push his buttons, and he found himself envying DC Calderwood's easy charm.

"Bloody toffs," he grumbled and lifted his binoculars up into the grey sky above Musselburgh Lagoons where five crows were mobbing a buzzard. Their sleek black feathers reminded him of academic gowns, and crows were certainly clever as well as brutal. The buzzard did not put up a fight but calmly glided into the trees to get away.

Chapter 11

Nobody likes Monday mornings, but McCord could not help thinking that by now he had more reason to hate them than most. As he pulled into Eglinton Crescent, he had a fair idea what he would find at number eighty-three. A small square in front of the entrance had been cordoned off, and crime scene officers, resembling astronauts in their white overalls and masks, were busy scanning the ground for evidence. Calderwood was waiting for him at the door, looking pale but without the green tinge; he must be getting used to spattered blood and brains.

"Zacharias Walker," he confirmed. "Same MO."

"When?"

"Dr Crane thinks late last night."

"Talk of the devil," McCord greeted the pathologist who appeared at the door, about to leave the premises. "Anything you can tell me?"

"You need to put an end to these bloody murders, McCord," Crane said. "Same MO as the last one. It's becoming a bit of a bore, isn't it? I can copy and paste half the report from last time. There is something mildly interesting, though."

"Yes?" McCord tried to suppress a desperate undertone in his voice.

"The victim seems to have attempted to write a message in his own blood. Remarkable, considering the state of his skull but then, in extreme situations, people do the most extraordinary things."

"What is the message?" McCord could barely conceal his impatience with the doctor's philosophising.

"Wouldn't like to guess," Crane answered. "Go see for yourself. You'll have my report this afternoon."

McCord inspected the door – solid wood, freshly painted in glossy black.

"No sign of forced entry," McCord observed. "Walker must have buzzed his killer in."

"So, he knew him," Calderwood concluded.

McCord just lifted his hands in a gesture that said: what have I been telling you all along?

They stepped into the hallway, ghostly lit by the halogen lamps of the forensic team. Off to their right was the frosted glass entrance to Zac Walker's stockbroker's business, straight ahead a solid stone staircase led up to the first floor flat.

"Who found him?" McCord asked as they were padding upstairs in their plastic overshoes.

"One of his employees," Calderwood told him. "When Walker didn't show up for work and didn't answer his mobile this morning, he went upstairs and rang the bell. When there was no answer, he found the neighbour who has a spare key."

They had reached the top of the stairs. A crime scene officer moved out of the way to let them into the flat.

"Have you interviewed the neighbour?" McCord asked Calderwood.

"He's in hospital under sedation – the shock, you see."

McCord saw.

The remains of Zacharias Walker lay face down on the floor, his feet near the door, and what was left of the head pointing towards the living room.

Forcing his instinctive revulsion to the back of his mind, McCord took in the scene. The right index finger of the dead man had drawn a few lines into his own blood – a wonky triangle ending in a broad smear where the hand had dropped and slid lifelessly across the wooden floorboards.

"An *A*," McCord declared at once. "Andrew Campbell."

Calderwood hesitated.

"It could be an unfinished *N* or *M* as well, maybe?"

"But the horizontal line?" McCord insisted. "It definitely looks like an *A* to me."

"It reaches only halfway across, and it is way down at the bottom. The man was dying; he would not have had control over his movements. It's a miracle that he managed to write as much as he did."

"You don't want it to be Andrew Campbell, do you?" McCord said accusingly. "You want Miss Thornton to be right, or rather, to be on the right side of Miss Thornton."

Calderwood blushed in a mixture of embarrassment and anger. "And you want Miss Thornton to be wrong," he retorted. "Maybe we should concentrate on the facts and the evidence instead?"

Despite his annoyance, McCord had to admit that his partner was right. He had committed the cardinal sin of policing – making assumptions fed by prejudice. He remembered his tutor at Tulliallan.

"Don't assume anything. Use your senses," she had told them once. "Look, listen, smell, and only then start thinking."

Look, he told himself. Look beyond what you expect or want to see.

"The footprint," McCord said.

Next to the body's head was a bloody footprint.

"It must be the killer's," Calderwood said. "Forensics have been all over it. If we find the shoe, we find the killer."

"It looks like a boot," McCord speculated. "But that's not what is interesting. Why is it *there*, next to the head? The killer waited for Walker to turn his back to him, bashed his head in, mission accomplished. Why would he step so far into the hall and risk leaving traces of himself behind?"

"You have a point," Calderwood conceded.

McCord stepped alongside the body until he stood close to where the killer had stood and looked around. He could see inside all the rooms from there: the study, the living room and the kitchen. What was he looking at? The rooms looked just the same as when he had been here last and talked to Walker. Maybe if he had told them everything, he would still be alive.

"We keep saying 'he'," McCord thought aloud, now questioning every single assumption he had ever made about this case.

"Well, we are looking for a very tall, strong person, are we not?" Calderwood asked.

"Maybe," McCord said.

He listened. The late morning traffic rumbled across the road outside but inside the flat there was no sound but the faint humming of the huge fridge freezer in the kitchen. He sniffed. So far, he had tried not to breathe in too deeply; the metallic smell of blood always made him nauseous. Now that he had stopped fighting the repugnant odour, he noticed something else.

"Pepperoni pizza," he declared.

"I don't know how you can think of lunch in a place like this," Calderwood said, sounding genuinely shocked. "I'm thinking of becoming a vegetarian, myself."

"You are an idiot, DC Calderwood," McCord said matter-of-factly. "Can't you smell it? There is a distinct whiff of pepperoni pizza about."

"Right," Calderwood said, looking offended.

"Go and have a look around and see if you can find the carton."

Calderwood carefully stepped past McCord and the mutilated body. "I wish I'd become a lawyer like Dad suggested," he muttered.

McCord, who had excellent hearing, shouted after Calderwood, who was darting in and out of every room. "Lawyers are the most hated profession in the world."

"When I think of the pay cheque and a nice office, I don't think I would mind," Calderwood replied.

"Yes, but where would have been the fun in that?"

After Calderwood had checked everywhere, even the bathroom, he returned to the hall. "Nothing. How odd."

"You're right," McCord said. "That's exactly what it is. Very odd indeed. And now we are going to see Mr Andrew Campbell before word gets out. Maybe another murder is going to loosen his tongue. And then we'll go back to the station to have a think."

* * *

"I've told you I want my lawyer present during any further interviews," Andrew Campbell said to them when McCord and Calderwood stepped into the hall of Carnethy House.

"And I told you that you are perfectly entitled to do that," McCord replied. "We can do this at the station with a lawyer present, but seeing that the station is surrounded by reporters, I thought you might prefer an informal chat here. Shall we go into the drawing room?"

Grudgingly, Andrew Campbell led the way. As they crossed the hall, Lucy joined them with a smile, mainly directed at the young detective constable.

"Tea? Coffee?" she offered.

"That won't be necessary," her employer snapped. "This is not going to take long."

Lucy shrugged apologetically towards the visitors and disappeared down the servants' staircase.

"So, what is it this time, Inspector?" Andrew Campbell asked after they had all sat down.

"There has been another murder," McCord said, watching their host's face closely as he spoke. "Another one of your old friends, Zacharias Walker."

This time Andrew Campbell was clearly taken aback.

"Zac?" he asked hoarsely. "How?"

"The same as the other two; a heavy blow to the head with a stone. Nothing of value taken, and we think that he probably knew the attacker because he opened the door to them."

For once, Andrew Campbell seemed to be lost for words.

McCord leaned forward.

"You understand my thinking now, Mr Campbell. Three out of a group of five close friends are now dead. If you are not the killer, it would be very wise to finally tell us what is going on here. We need to stop this madness."

"I don't know!" Andrew Campbell burst out. "I have no idea what is going on!"

"Right," said McCord, his face hardening. "Let's start with Mr Walker's business proposition to you and your friends. Are you still insisting that it was nothing but a high-risk investment, which upset Mr McArthur so much that he started an argument with Mr Walker?"

Andrew Campbell sighed.

"I suppose this is all going to come out now anyway. Zac was involved in some insider dealing. He never said much about it, but he made too much money too quickly for it to be legit. During that shooting weekend, he offered us a chance to invest. He knew of a start-up company that was about to be taken over by Google. The shares would have rocketed a few days later. It was a stupid thing to suggest. Robbie had gone all respectable after he got married and had the baby, Alex can't shift a penny without his wife's say-so, and I don't have any money to invest. Maybe he thought we would be impressed. He was always a bit… needy."

"It would have helped immensely if you had told us this earlier, Mr Campbell," McCord said sternly. "Do you know if Mr McArthur was about to expose Mr Walker's criminal activities?"

Andrew Campbell shrugged.

"He was angry, but I'm not sure. I don't see how it matters now. It would have given Zac a motive for killing Robbie, but who killed Zac?"

"Well, maybe somebody did get involved in the insider dealing. Covering up criminal activity is a powerful motive for murder. Are you sure we won't find any of your money tied up in Mr Walker's accounts?" McCord asked.

Andrew Campbell laughed mirthlessly.

"If you find any, please let me know. There's a pile of unpaid bills in the office."

McCord did not look sympathetic in the least. "Where were you last night?"

"I was here having dinner on my own because Mama was out. No witnesses, I'm afraid."

"That is a great pity," McCord said. "Goodbye, Mr Campbell."

Chapter 12

On the way out, McCord checked his watch.

"Coffee time," he said to Calderwood, nodding in the direction of the estate manager's office.

Justin Torrence was washing his hands over the sink.

There was an odd smell in the room. Seeing McCord frown, he pointed to one of the estate's hounds, who was lying on a rug, unconscious but breathing deeply and regularly. One of the paws was thickly bandaged.

"It was a nasty cut, so she had to have a little operation. She'll come round in a minute."

He dried his hands and held up a shard of glass.

"People can be so inconsiderate," he said.

"Mr Torrence," McCord began, "we need to ask you a few questions."

"Again?" he asked. "Mrs Campbell will not be pleased when she hears that you have been back. What do you need to know this time?"

"You told us that Mr Campbell was on the estate last Monday morning. Are you absolutely sure about that? It is important," said McCord.

Torrence threw the shard into the bin.

"Yes, I'm sure."

"And what about last night? Did you see Mr Campbell last night?"

"Sort of."

"What do you mean, sort of?" McCord asked.

"His car was here, and there was a light on in his room. I came back around nine from checking on the hounds when I saw his silhouette moving across the room."

"That couldn't have been Mrs Campbell?" asked McCord. "Or Lucy taking something to his room?"

Torrence's mouth twitched.

"I see what you're getting at, but I *am* able to tell the difference between Mr Campbell's and a woman's shadow."

McCord nodded, defeated. "Thank you, Mr Torrence. Your assistance is very much appreciated. Goodbye."

Torrence made a non-committal gesture as if to say, 'no big deal'.

"Any time."

* * *

"A nice chap, and very observant. But I suppose nothing much happens around here, so things would be noticed," Calderwood remarked as they were driving towards Carnethy village. "Without Torrence's alibi, Andrew Campbell would be in real trouble. Surely, the DNA from the cigarette stub has come back by now; maybe that will give us a breakthrough."

McCord nodded. "Let's hope so."

On the main road, McCord slowed down and parked in front of the post office. He had gone without a cigarette for six months and without nicotine gums for three, but every so often a sudden craving threatened to overwhelm him.

"I need some chewing gum," he told Calderwood, "and while I'm getting that, you can use your upper-class charm to get some of the local gossip about the Campbells."

McCord quickly found the gum, but seeing that Calderwood was already in deep conversation with the woman behind the till, he began browsing amongst the magazines, all the while listening to what was being said about the 'big house'.

"...and money isn't everything, is it," the postmistress was saying. "Doesn't mean that they are any better than you and me. Mind you, the older son seems nice enough, he was in here once. But the younger one is a right scoundrel if you ask me. Lucy, their housekeeper, a nice girl, she has no time for them either."

"So why does she work for them then?" Calderwood asked.

"It's her dad, you see," the postmistress explained. "He's quite poorly, so Lucy needs to look after him, and there aren't many jobs around here. She was quite excited when she first got the position; she thought she was moving up in the world, but that soon changed."

Calderwood was all ears. "Why, what happened?"

The postmistress clearly relished having an audience.

"Well, she never told me, but her dad said she came home all upset one evening. She didn't want to talk about it, and he told her to quit, but she didn't. I've been wondering if she fancies that estate manager, she mentions him a lot. I wonder how he is getting on up there. It was funny how he got the job. Lucy told me all this, but I'm prattling on – are you sure you want to hear all this?"

"Absolutely, do tell," Calderwood humoured her.

"He was in here first, looking for a job as a handyman. He had heard in the local pub that the estate was pretty run down, so on the off-chance he turned up at the big house. Mrs Campbell was just leaving to go into town, but her car wouldn't start. He offered to help and got the car going in no time and refused to take any money. Mrs Campbell was really impressed, so he asked her if they needed any staff, and she said yes! How funny is that? Sometimes you just get lucky. Mind you, I don't know if he *was* lucky to get the job. But I suppose he gets his lodgings for free, and Lucy says, he never complains. He keeps himself to himself, so being out here on his own doesn't seem to bother him. Are you okay over there, my dear?" she shouted across to McCord.

Feeling guilty, he grabbed a magazine at random and put it on the counter, together with several packets of spearmint gum. It was only when he saw the postmistress's surprised look and Calderwood's grin that he noticed what the magazine was – *Tatler.* He threw a ten-pound note on the little tray, picked up his purchases with the change and fled.

Outside, Calderwood pointed to the magazine. He could not stop laughing.

"That'll give you all the latest gossip on high fashion and the upper classes," he gasped.

"Shut up and get into the car," McCord grumbled. "It was interesting, what the postmistress said. I wonder what happened to Lucy up at the estate. Maybe we should get Amy onto that; she is good at that sort of thing. Lucy also started her job not long before Jordan Lamond was murdered, so she might well have met him as well. We need to sit down and think all this through systematically. Something is staring us in the face and we're just not seeing it."

* * *

The proposed thinking session had to be delayed, however, because Superintendent Gilchrist was expecting McCord in his office.

"What is going on, DI McCord?" the Super blustered without even a perfunctory greeting.

"*Three* unsolved murders on your patch – the newspapers will be full of it!"

"With all due respect, sir," McCord replied, "the last one only happened last night."

"Still – there are rumours of a serial killer bashing people's heads in! This is not good PR for us!"

McCord swallowed the obvious 'even less good for the victims' but realised he did not have much to offer his boss by way of consolation. What *did* they have?

"The only connection between the victims we can find is that they all went to university together. They seem to have been a tight-knit group around that time. We've been interviewing the other members of that group, Alexander Buchan and Andrew Campbell, but could not make anything stick."

The Super was aghast.

"Andrew Campbell? Of the Carnethy Estate? Brother of John Campbell, the proprietor of *Forth Write* magazine?"

"The very same, sir."

"Are you out of your mind, DI McCord? Accusing a member of one of the most illustrious families in Edinburgh of being a deranged serial killer?"

"We are not accusing anybody yet; we're just gathering background information."

"'Gathering background information'? You're supposed to be chasing a killer! How many times have you been up at the estate to interrogate Mr Campbell?"

"Three times," McCord admitted.

The Super choked on his saliva and started to cough.

"Three times! That is not gathering background information, that is harassment! The assistant chief constable used to play golf with the late Mr Campbell, and no doubt, his widow will be in touch. Oh, dear God!"

Gilchrist slumped back into his leather chair, already forming in his mind the reply to the complaint coming his way.

"There is no reason for her to complain. On the contrary, I have warned Andrew Campbell that he might well be in danger if his former university friends are being killed off one by one."

This did not improve the Super's mood.

"Are you telling me you are expecting more murder victims? And that Mr Campbell could be one of them? Have you thought of offering Mr Campbell protection? And the other gentleman as well, of course?"

"Not yet, sir."

It occurred to McCord that a protection officer would be able to keep an eye on Andrew Campbell as well as protect him.

"Well, why are you still here?" Gilchrist demanded. "This lunatic has done away with three alumni of Edinburgh University! By the way, how is young

Calderwood shaping up? You're not suspecting him of murder as well, are you?" He laughed at his own attempt at humour.

"He is doing very well, sir. An excellent choice. A real asset to the force."

The Super seemed a little mollified.

"That's at least something. Right, why are you still standing around here? You have a serial killer to catch!"

"Yes, sir," McCord said and, swearing under his breath, returned to his office.

Chapter 13

When Amy came back from lunch, John waved her into the office.

"My mother has been on the phone. She says the police were up at the estate again. She is furious that they took a DNA sample from Andrew but haven't told him yet about the result. They asked if he had an alibi, and thankfully, Justin was once again able to provide him with one. I do not know what we would do without him. Andrew might have been arrested by now."

"Try not to worry," Amy said. "They have nothing on him; it's just that DI McCord has got it into his head that Andrew is at the centre of this. I've heard that his boss has warned him off already and suggested police protection."

"Andrew would never agree to that, I am sure. Can you imagine him going round with a police officer in tow, cramping his style?" John shook his head. "It is exactly the fact that DI McCord suspects him that worries me. DI McCord is a very shrewd man; what if he is right?"

"He is not," Amy said decisively.

"Well, if he is not, then Andrew is possibly in danger. So, whichever way you look at it, the situation is dire. Have you seen the dailies this morning?" He pointed to the tabloid headlines on his screen. "SERIAL KILLER ON THE LOOSE IN EDINBURGH, THE ROCK KILLER STRIKES AGAIN, and so it goes on. Ruth McCowan writes in her piece for *The Morning Herald*, with some glee, I must say, that for the first time in her career, a serial killer is targeting men rather than women, and she has found out about the university connection. She mentions Alexander Buchan and Andrew as members of a close-knit group, at the time famous, or notorious according to her, for their bohemian lifestyle. She has been pestering Mama for an interview – without success, of course. I fear, however, that the press will be camping out on the lawn soon. My phone has not stopped ringing either since then. What *are* we to do with the Saturday edition? We cannot possibly keep pretending this is not happening."

"The obvious solution is to find the killer," Amy said. "I've been asking around about Alexander Buchan, and I get the impression he is a man with secrets as well as a bad temper. He comes from a wealthy family and after graduating, worked for his father but left a year later. Rumour has it that his father threw him out and disinherited him because he used some of the company's funds for his own benefit. He then started the estate agent's business but barely scraped a living until he married his current wife. It seems that she's the one with the money and has invested in the business. Her money and his connections then secured him some big property deals."

"There is nothing criminal or even immoral in that," John pointed out. "And he found another potential buyer for your mum's flat who seems very interested, so it is not all bad."

"True, but could you believe how enthusiastic he was about the shop when the buyer was there on Monday? Have you ever seen such a liar? If I hadn't been there myself on Saturday, I could have sworn he was genuine. I have the impression that he is the kind of guy who can be tempted into some dodgy dealing. If he is as much under his wife's thumb as people say, he might be desperate to have some money of his own. He has a lot to lose if there is something she mustn't find out. That he is still in love with Cheryl Langley, now Gibbs, for example. Or that he did get involved in some insider dealing with Zac Walker."

John looked sceptical.

"Fine, go with it, but be careful. If you are right, he could be a dangerous man."

There was a knock on the door.

Martin came in and placed a couple of mochaccinos on John's desk. "I thought you could do with some refreshments," he said.

"Any news on the murders?" he asked Amy with a side glance at John.

"I'm just on my way to dig into the background of one of the suspects," Amy said. "Thanks for the coffee, but I must be off."

As she stood up, her phone fell off her lap and slid across the floor. Solicitously, Martin moved across the room and bent his tall, lanky frame to pick it up. As Amy looked down on his thinning crown, she had a lightbulb moment. She grabbed her phone from Martin's hand and dialled McCord's number.

* * *

McCord groaned. His 'thinking' time had led to no further insights into the psyche of the killer. Both Andrew Campbell and Alexander Buchan had emphatically declined the offer of police protection, which was a relief since he did not have the manpower to follow them around all day anyway. On the other hand, it made him think that both had something to hide. His only hope rested on the PM report that was about to arrive any time now. When the display of his phone showed Amy's name, he groaned again and pressed the green button.

"What's up?" he asked.

"I'm very well, too, thank you," Amy said pointedly. "I know how the killer got up to Robert McArthur's head. No need to look for a giant, anybody could have done it."

McCord waved Calderwood over and put Amy on speaker phone.

"The killer put a phone on the ground and waited for McArthur to come jogging along. When McArthur was close enough, the killer called the phone to make it light up and ring. McArthur bent down to look at the phone – everybody would have done that – and bang."

McCord listened with a mixture of delight at her insight and annoyance that he had not thought of this himself.

"Thank you," McCord said when Amy had finished. "Yes, occasionally your ideas are very good."

He laughed at her snort.

"By the way," Amy continued, "*The Morning Herald* has devoted its front page to the serial killer and made the connection to a certain group of men from Edinburgh University. Andrew's name is mentioned. The other papers are bound to follow, so the Campbells are in for a rough time. Mrs Campbell is on the war path trying to protect her son and has been talking about contacting the assistant chief constable. You'd better watch out."

McCord sighed. "Damn hacks. I sometimes wish…"

"Careful now," Amy warned, albeit with a smile in her voice. "Although I seem to spend more time investigating your case, I'm still a member of the self-same press."

"Yes, but that's different." He was about to add something but noticed Calderwood's expression.

"Keep me posted," was all he said before he hung up.

"I see now why you let Amy in here," Calderwood teased him. "She is right; the killer didn't need to be tall or strong to kill Robbie McArthur, they just needed to be very clever."

McCord nodded approvingly.

"And he – or she – probably used the same trick with Walker. Dropped a phone or something else on the floor, which slid along the hall, and when Walker turned and bent down to pick it up, they killed him. But then, they had to step further into the hall to pick up whatever it was they had dropped."

"It is odd, though, that the killer thought they had to do that," Calderwood said. "If Walker knew the killer and trusted them enough to let them into the flat, surely, he would have turned his back on them anyway as he went ahead into the living room or the study."

"Good point," McCord conceded. He put himself back into the flat; the footprint, the humming of the fridge, the smell of blood and pepperoni… McCord banged the table.

"I am such an idiot. Which strangers do we open our doors to, Calderwood?"

"Delivery drivers!" Calderwood exclaimed. "I'll check the pizza places closest to Eglinton Crescent and see what Walker ordered and who delivered it."

He rushed back to his desk and woke up his computer to follow their new lead. McCord could not bear to sit around idly, so he called the lab again.

"Any news on the cigarette stub?" he demanded. The voice on the other end launched into a lengthy explanation.

"Damn. And the rocks?"

Another lecture, this time on the various properties of rock.

"Thanks," McCord said eventually. "Please email me the report once you're finished."

Calderwood looked up from his internet search. "Anything?"

"Yes and no. The cigarette stub was damp from the dew and so there is no conclusive match to Andrew Campbell's DNA. It would not be enough for a conviction, but it does not score him off our list of suspects either."

"And the rocks?" Calderwood asked.

"Both the rocks found at the murder scenes come from the same place. Not Arthur's Seat or anywhere in Edinburgh. The closest the guy could think of are the Pentland Hills."

"Which is where the Campbell's estate is," Calderwood said, finishing McCord's sentence. "All circumstantial, but isn't it odd how all clues lead back to Andrew Campbell?"

McCord nodded.

"Very odd indeed."

Chapter 14

Amy unlocked the door of the old flat with mixed feelings. It seemed silly to come back when the new place in Queen Street was piled high with all her stuff randomly thrown into boxes and binbags, and she had no idea which contained the bedding she was going to use that night, or her toothbrush, for that matter. The move had been a swirl of utter chaos. Valerie was busy moving into John's flat, and never having lived on her own, Amy had felt lonely and displaced. After sitting for an hour listening to the silence, she had decided to go back to say goodbye properly to her childhood home.

The previous buyer had delayed yet again and the new one had not committed to anything either, so the flat and shop lay empty and deserted. Valerie was worried sick about the bridging loan she had to take out, but thank God she had John, whose calming presence helped her see things in proportion and gave her the wonderful feeling that everything would be fine.

Amy turned the key and entered the dark hallway. The sound of the door closing behind her echoed through the flat, and she quickly switched on the light. The marks on the wall showed where their pictures had hung. The kitchen – where she had sat every afternoon telling her mum all the news from school while wolfing down a hastily prepared snack before Valerie had to rush back down to the shop – lay there, stripped of the life that had been lived within it. The sitting room, where they had cuddled up on the sofa and watched movies together, was nothing but an empty space with the imprints of the furniture on the carpet as the only signs that people had once filled it with chatter and laughter.

Amy wondered if it was like saying goodbye to somebody who had died but finding only a shell with the soul departed. She shivered and decided never to view the body of a loved one but to remember them as they were when still alive. No, this part of her life was over, and she must embrace the next.

She locked up again and was descending the metal staircase to the ground floor when she thought she heard a noise from the shop. She must have imagined it; who would break into empty premises? Kids? But as she walked down the outside stairs, she knew she would not have any peace of mind until she had checked. Shivering in the fierce wind which was howling through the gaps in the metal steps, she pulled the keys out of her handbag again and tried to unlock the door. The key would not turn, and it took her a second to realise that the door was already open. Maybe her mum had forgotten to lock up before jumping into the removal van; that would be just like her.

Her hand found the light switch next to the entrance with blind confidence but when she pressed it, nothing happened. Nervous now, she moved slowly into the room, listening and waiting for her eyes to adapt to the dim light. The streetlamp opposite and the headlights of passing cars threw fleeting, orange-coloured shapes onto the walls that gave the illusion of other-worldly creatures moving around the room. A beam of light illuminated an oblong, three-dimensional shape on the floor. Her curiosity had given way to fear as she edged closer to the strange object.

A floorboard creaked behind her, but before she could turn round, a cloth was pressed over her mouth.

Helplessly, she clawed at the hand that stopped her from breathing and kicked the legs behind her, until the beams of light danced in front of her eyes and dissolved into darkness.

* * *

McCord and his father were working their way through a tasty lamb pasanda when Keith McCord nodded towards the photograph of a woman that stood on the mantlepiece.

"It is the anniversary of your mum's death next week. Shall we go to Mortonhall, and then for a nice dinner afterwards?"

McCord automatically agreed. He knew how important these occasions were for his dad, who loved to point to his wife's name in the book listing the dead and to stroll through the Garden of Remembrance. Under the old trees he would tell McCord stories about his mother, who had died giving birth to him. McCord found these occasions increasingly painful. Having no memories of his mother but the ones created by his father, these stories of a bright, vivacious young woman compounded his sense of loss rather than alleviating it. His mother was a ghost, a phantom, perfect but insubstantial and beyond reach. When he looked up, he saw that his father was observing him closely.

"It is such a tragedy that you never got to meet her," Keith McCord said. "I've been trying to bring her to life for you but I'm not sure I can. And I wonder sometimes," he added after some hesitation, "whether this is why you are struggling with relationships."

"I'm not struggling with relationships," McCord bristled. "I just haven't found the right person yet."

"You'll never find the right person if you're looking for perfection," Keith said.

"For you, Mum was perfect, wasn't she? You've never looked at another woman since."

Keith sighed. "That's true, but I'm beginning to wonder if that was fair on you. I should have at least tried to find a nice step-mother for you."

"Good God," McCord exclaimed, horrified. "Don't even think about it. "What would I do without our curry and chess nights?"

Just then his work phone rang.

"Yes?"

"We've got him, sir, we've got him! You were right all along." Calderwood sounded as if he was bouncing up and down while he was speaking.

McCord was not entirely sure what 'right' meant because recently he had been doubting everything he had ever assumed about this case.

"Calm down, man," he admonished his partner. "You're not making sense. Just start from the beginning."

Calderwood took a deep breath.

"Uniform was alerted to a break-in on South Bridge. When they arrived, they found Andrew Campbell kneeling over the body of Alexander Buchan, blood all over him. Same MO, same type of rock."

"Yes!" McCord punched the air. "Has he confessed?"

"No, he keeps ranting and shouting that he is innocent, but then he would, wouldn't he? Four brutal murders; he'll never see daylight again."

McCord thought of Amy and John, and what it would do to them, and any feeling of triumph dissipated.

"I'll be right over. Wait for the interview until I'm there."

"Of course, sir. Just hurry!"

McCord killed the call.

"They've caught Andrew Campbell at the scene of another murder."

"Then why are you looking so glum?" his father asked.

"All the time I was after him and part of me wanted it to be him, but now I wish it was somebody different," McCord explained.

"That wouldn't have anything to do with the fact that he is sort of a family member of that girl Amy you've been mentioning?"

"Maybe it has," McCord said curtly, not wanting to get into another conversation about the women, or the lack thereof, in his life. "But even so, somehow it doesn't sit right."

Keith McCord smiled at his son.

"Your instinct has always been good, Russell," he said. "Better to be sure; after all, it's the rest of a man's life you're talking about."

McCord grabbed his car keys, affectionately squeezed his dad's shoulder, and rushed out to his Juke.

* * *

At the station, the PC who had been first on the scene was waiting to brief him. There had been an anonymous call to report a burglary on South Bridge, but when they arrived, they had found the body of Alexander Buchan and Andrew Campbell kneeling beside it. It was obvious that the young man could not believe his luck.

"We've arrested Mr Campbell, who initially resisted, and called forensics to secure the murder scene."

McCord, who had heard all this already from Calderwood, was not listening.

"What was the address again?" he asked abruptly.

"South Bridge, number" – he checked his notes – "sixty-five. The boutique called Valerie's."

It took McCord a lot of effort to keep his voice calm.

"When you got to the murder scene, where were the ladies who live at that address?"

The PC looked confused.

"Nobody lives there, sir. The shop was completely empty. We rang the bell upstairs but there was an 'under offer' sign outside, and there was nobody in. From the outside we saw that the curtains had gone; the neighbours said they had moved out earlier that day."

McCord breathed a sigh of relief.

"Thank you, Constable. Good night."

* * *

The Andrew Campbell sitting in Interview Room 2 bore no resemblance to his former self. His face grey, shining with sweat, trembling hands gripping the edge of the melamine table, he had lost all the self-assurance that until now had seemed an essential part of his nature.

"It wasn't me!" he shouted as soon as McCord entered the room. "You have to believe me!"

Ignoring him, McCord turned to Calderwood who stood next to the door with his arms folded as if to indicate that it was no use trying to escape or make excuses.

"Has he been cautioned?"

"Yes, and he called his brother. Apparently, a lawyer is on his way."

"Excellent," McCord said although he did not feel happy at all. "While we're waiting, Mr Campbell, you can contemplate the prospect of life imprisonment without parole versus a very long prison sentence but with a chance to eat in a restaurant again at some point. Maybe. It all depends on how cooperative you are and how much remorse you demonstrate. Claiming that you're innocent when you've been caught next to the fourth victim in a series of identical murders is not going to look good to a judge."

"But I can't admit to something I haven't done! I'm innocent! I–"

A knock on the door interrupted him.

A genteel-looking elderly gentleman entered the room and surveyed the occupants with a shrewd glance.

"Ah, Mr Campbell. I hear from your brother that you are in a spot of bother. I hope you haven't started without me, DI McCord?" he said to the inspector. "Your reputation precedes you," he added when McCord looked surprised. "Alan Cooper, pleased to meet you."

They shook hands, and McCord introduced Calderwood to the brief.

Mr Cooper, whose long, thin neck and tufty white bushes of hair reminded McCord of a great crested grebe, pulled out a pristine notepad and an expensive-looking pen and sat next to his client, patting him reassuringly on the arm.

"I hope DI McCord has not been upsetting you with vague threats of a life sentence?" he asked Andrew Campbell. "Because that would have been very naughty considering we haven't even heard your side of the story yet."

McCord understood the warning, and concluded that for all his unperturbed serenity, Mr Cooper was no walk-over.

"Well, let's hear your side of the story then," McCord said and switched on the tape.

After the usual spiel detailing the date, time and names of the people present, he turned to Andrew Campbell.

"Mr Campbell, can you tell us how you came to be found kneeling next to the body of Mr Alexander Buchan earlier this evening?"

Andrew Campbell swallowed, his eyes darting between his lawyer and the detective who had been on his trail ever since the murder of Robbie McArthur.

"I got a text message from Alex this evening, asking me to meet him at an address on South Bridge. It said, 'I know who the killer is, got something you need to see.' I was in town anyway, so I went over straightaway. When I got there, the door was open, and the lights were on.

At first, I couldn't see anybody but then I looked behind the counter. And there he was – dead."

He started retching but Calderwood shot a sceptical glance in McCord's direction. Play-acting, the look said.

"Why didn't you call the police? Why did you kneel next to the body and get blood all over yourself?" McCord asked.

"His head was covered with a cloth. I thought it was him, but I was not sure, and I wondered if he was still alive. I nudged him but he didn't move. Then I took the cloth away, and saw that it was him with his head…" His voice trailed off.

McCord frowned.

"Why did you not take the cloth off first to see who it was?"

Andrew Campbell looked confused. "I don't know, why, I…"

"Maybe he was afraid of what he would find underneath the cloth," Mr Cooper gently interjected. "Most of us are not as hardened to mutilated bodies as you are, DI McCord."

McCord ignored that last remark.

"My question remains, why not call the police?" he asked Andrew Campbell who looked even more confused.

"Because by the time I had taken in what had happened, your lot were already there."

Mr Cooper cleared his throat.

"This is a very plausible account of what happened, don't you think, DI McCord? Mr Buchan found out who the killer was and alerted my client, but the killer got to him before Mr Campbell arrived."

"I'm afraid I find it a lot less plausible than you do," McCord said. "This is the fourth murder committed with pieces of rock commonly found on Mr Campbell's estate. We have a cigarette stub that was dropped on the morning of Mr McArthur's murder right next to the scene of the crime, which is the same brand that your client smokes, and–"

"Let me stop you right there," Mr Cooper interjected. "Was the DNA on the stub a match to my client's DNA?"

McCord's lips were a thin line.

"Not conclusively, no, but the result suggests that it is quite possible–"

"'Quite possible' is not going to get you very far in court, is it, DI McCord. And anybody can pick up rocks in the Pentland Hills. Is there anything else that is more substantial?"

"The third victim drew an *A* into his own blood before he died," McCord said.

Mr Cooper seemed to ponder this.

"Hmm, interesting. I see where you are coming from. But tell me, how many names start with an *A*? Adam? Alan? Maybe he meant me?" He raised his eyebrows as if to say that there was no end of silly scenarios. "Maybe he did not want to tell us the name of his killer but convey another message? Who knows?"

His serene smile began to get on McCord's nerves.

"I also believe," the lawyer continued, "that Mr Campbell has alibis for two of the four murders you are accusing him of, and I understand that you are working on the assumption that all the murders were committed by the same person?"

"I'll be interviewing the witness again," McCord said through clenched teeth. "Maybe Mr Campbell has been paying him or putting him under pressure. We'll look into that, trust me."

"That is your prerogative," Mr Cooper said cheerfully. "Another thing I've been wondering about is Mr Campbell's motive. Why would he murder four of his oldest friends?"

"That we will find out as well," McCord said. "And until then, Mr Campbell will be Her Majesty's guest."

The lawyer rose.

"You have a lot to do in the next twenty-four hours, DI McCord. After that, I am quite confident that Mr Campbell will be able to return home a free man."

He patted Andrew Campbell encouragingly on the shoulder, and the gesture reminded McCord of himself and his dad. This lawyer had probably had ties with the family for decades, and he certainly was a formidable ally to the Campbells.

In the corridor, Mr Cooper waited until Andrew had been led away to the cells and Calderwood was out of earshot before he turned to McCord.

"If I were you, I would not waste a full day trying to prove Andrew's guilt; your time would be better spent looking elsewhere. But then, I have the advantage of having known this young man from when he was born. And while he might not be the most respectable of citizens, I am convinced that he is not guilty of those murders. For one thing, he is simply too lazy, and for the other" – he lowered his voice to a whisper – "he is not bright enough. Good luck, DI McCord, with finding the real killer before he strikes again."

* * *

Calderwood was waiting impatiently for McCord in their office.

"Sutton wants to see you."

McCord rushed over and knocked on the outer wall of her workstation.

"Come in," came the answer from within.

"What have you got, DC Sutton?"

Her eyes were fixed on the screen.

"Zacharias Walker, phone records. Got a call from William Gibbs two days before his death."

"I'll be damned," McCord thought aloud. "Could all this be about Cheryl Gibbs after all?"

DC Sutton shrugged.

"Look into the email exchanges between Lamond, McArthur, Walker, Buchan, Campbell and Cheryl Langley around the time of the assault," McCord said. "I'll try to get a warrant asap but start straight away."

Without a word, DC Sutton began to type.

Back at his desk, McCord pulled out the witness statements from William and Cheryl Gibbs. "We need to follow this up," he told Calderwood. "If Gibbs is our killer, Andrew Campbell could be in danger when we have to release him."

"But why would William Gibbs have a grudge against them all?" Calderwood wondered. "It must be connected to the abortion, surely."

"Maybe we've looked at this the wrong way," McCord said. "Maybe there are different killers. Gibbs' alibi for McArthur's murder is weak, and here he would have a clear and strong motive. Check his alibi for Zac Walker's murder. And what if he and his wife are in this together? We never even contemplated her as a suspect. What the hell happened at Edinburgh Uni seven years ago?"

"We need to interview Gibbs again and ask him about the phone call," Calderwood suggested.

"Yes, but I don't want to scare him off before Sutton has a chance to unearth some evidence. And luckily, we have somebody right here who knows all about this affair."

When the door of his cell was opened, Andrew Campbell immediately got to his feet.

"About time," he whined, his old arrogance resurfacing. "Can I go now?"

"Oh no," McCord replied. "First, you are going to tell me what exactly happened around the time Cheryl Gibbs, or Langley as she was then, fell pregnant."

"What do you mean, 'happened'?" Andrew Campbell sneered. "I would have thought you were aware of the facts of life?"

McCord's patience was wearing thin.

"Can I remind you that you are still our prime suspect, and even if we don't find a motive, the circumstances will be enough to convict you in the eyes of a jury, no matter what your lawyer says?"

Chastened, Andrew Campbell sat back on the thin mattress of the cell bed.

"Believe it or not, I wasn't in the room when they had sex. I'm not into that sort of thing. Why don't you ask her?"

"We will, don't worry," McCord said. "I just thought you might want to help us investigate other leads, but please yourself."

* * *

Returning to his office, McCord realised it was past midnight. After the initial buzz, the station had calmed down. A colleague had conveyed the news of Alexander Buchan's death to his wife, who tearfully professed to have no idea why anybody, Andrew Campbell or otherwise, would want her husband dead. There was nothing to be done until the morning when reports of door-to-door enquiries, witness statements and forensic results would be coming in.

Calderwood had gone home to his flat in Stockbridge to watch some cricket after leaving a note that none of the pizza joints in the west end had a record of an order for Zacharias Walker. McCord's mind, however, was on the most recent murder, so he left the note in the Walker file to think about later. His bet was still on Andrew Campbell, and the top priority now was to crack his alibi, but he would also have to interview William and Cheryl Gibbs as a matter of urgency. First, though, he needed a few hours of sleep.

Chapter 15

When Amy came to, rough fabric was scratching her cheek. Where was she? She waited for her eyes to adjust to the darkness, but nothing happened. Not even vague contours emerged from the utter blackness around her. Had she gone blind? But then she remembered. Someone had attacked her in the shop. Where had they taken her? Drowsy and nauseous, she lifted her head and touched the ground next to her. A woollen blanket on a mat. Suppressing the rising feeling of panic, she got onto her knees and ran her fingers over her surroundings. Another blanket that her kidnapper had covered her with. Pushing it aside, she tried to make sense of what her fingertips told her.

The floor was compacted earth, and next to her mat, she found what felt like a flask and a plastic bag. Inside, she guessed from the materials and sounds, were packets of biscuits, crisps and several water bottles. The next thing took her longer to identify. A parcel wrapped in aluminium foil. Blindly, she opened it and smelt ham. She prodded the contents of the parcel – definitely a sandwich. Still feeling sick from the anaesthetic but encouraged by the thought that her kidnapper apparently did not want her to perish from cold or starvation, she patted down the foil again and widened the circle of her exploration. Her knees were beginning to hurt, so she stood up slowly. She stretched out her hands and touched a rough, vaulted stone ceiling, just above her head, which seamlessly turned into walls.

How airless this dungeon was! The panic rose again, and she struggled to breathe. Frantically, she kept feeling her way along the wall. There must be an opening somewhere! Eventually, the surface changed. Wood. A heavy wooden door. Nothing else. She examined every inch of the door with her fingers but could not find any lock. It must have been bolted from the outside. A storage space in a cellar? Between the door and the wall, where they did not quite meet, she felt a faint draught. She pressed her nose against the gap and breathed in deeply. At least she would not suffocate. She banged against the door and screamed at the top of her voice, but apart from hurting her hands and becoming hoarse, she achieved nothing.

Shivering with cold, she crawled back to her makeshift bed and wrapped herself in the blanket again. What was happening to her? She tried to remember what she had seen before she passed out. A bulky shape on the floor, a strange, metallic smell... Her stomach lurched. The fourth victim of the serial killer? But who? And why was it in her mum's shop? The only connection they had was Alexander Buchan. Andrew? Had he brought her here? That would explain the attempts to make her a little more comfortable in her prison cell. But what were his plans for her? How could he let her go if he was on the run; and if he had been caught, why hadn't he told the police where she was? He must be insane to have killed all these people. Her lungs seemed to go into spasm. 'Calm down,' she told herself. She had to stay awake and figure out what it all meant. She had to be ready for him when he came back. But drowsiness threatened to overwhelm her; the bulky shape on the floor of the shop, the move, the attack all blended into a random sequence of flashbacks, and seconds later she drifted back into unconsciousness.

* * *

If Edith Campbell had been cold towards McCord up to this point, she was now openly hostile.

"You are not welcome here, DI McCord," she announced as he and Calderwood entered the hall of Carnethy House the following morning. "You have thrown my innocent boy into prison after endlessly harassing him, and now you are back again. What else do you want? To arrest me as well?"

"I want the truth," McCord said, quite indifferent to her accusations, "and I think somebody here has been telling lies. Where is your estate manager?"

"I have no idea. What has he got to do with anything?"

"He is a key witness, and I need to speak to him again. Now, please."

Calderwood, clearly uncomfortable with McCord's tone towards the lady of the house, intervened.

"Mrs Campbell, your son was found next to the fourth body in a recent string of similar murders. We had no choice but to arrest him. If he is indeed innocent, which I hope we will be able to prove, he could well be the next intended victim, and a police station is probably the safest place for him. The sooner we solve these murders, the sooner your son will be home."

With a reluctant gesture, Edith Campbell invited them into the drawing room.

"Thank you very much; hopefully, it won't take long," said McCord, attempting to emulate his DC's diplomatic stance.

"I believe he is in his office," Edith Campbell said. "Lucy!" she called into the hall where the housekeeper was passing carrying a coal bucket. "Tell Justin to come here immediately, and then bring us some tea."

Lucy dropped the bucket and hurried off to find the estate manager.

"Does he know what happened last night?" McCord asked.

"Yes, he was here this morning and saw that I was upset, so I told him. It's not in the papers yet, but it will be this evening, I'm sure. Vultures," Edith Campbell added with venom.

"Absolutely appalling," Calderwood agreed hastily. "The best thing is to ignore them; it will all blow over soon."

"The shame," she whispered, "to see the family name dragged through the papers like this, and all for nothing. I daren't go to town anymore."

Through the open door, they saw Lucy reappear with the worried-looking estate manager. Reluctantly, he followed Edith Campbell's order to sit down.

"Mr Torrence," McCord began, "I think you are aware that we arrested Andrew Campbell at the scene of a murder last night. He was kneeling next to the body and is now the main suspect in a multiple murder inquiry. Bearing that in mind, would you like to revise your statements regarding Mr Campbell's whereabouts during the murders of Robert McArthur and Zacharias Walker?"

The estate manager perched on the sofa with a stricken face but said nothing.

"Stop bullying him," Edith Campbell demanded. "If he said Andrew was here, he was here. Which he was, anyway, I keep telling you."

"Mr Torrence," McCord persisted, ignoring the host's outburst, "perverting the course of justice carries a prison sentence of two years, and, as things stand, you could well be found to be an accessory to multiple murders, which would be much, much more serious. You are an honest man, and I'd hate to see you go down protecting somebody entirely unworthy of your sacrifice. Has he paid you? Or put you under any kind of pressure?"

"How dare you!" spluttered Edith Campbell. "You…"

"Please don't upset yourself, ma'am," Calderwood intervened. "DI McCord is only doing his job. It is in Mr Torrence's as well as your son's interest that we finally get to the truth."

The estate manager glanced apologetically at his employer.

"I am sorry," he said finally, both to her and McCord. "I don't know whether Mr Campbell was here during the times you asked me about. I didn't see him leave but I couldn't swear he was here, either."

"Well," McCord said, his voice a mix of triumph and exasperation, "it might have prevented the last murder if you had been telling the truth from the start. What exactly did Mr Campbell do to persuade you to give a false statement to the police in a murder inquiry?"

"He did nothing!" the estate manager exclaimed. "Nothing of the sort. I owe the Campbell family so much. They gave me a job when I most needed it even when I was not exactly qualified for it. I was sure, eh, I *am* sure that Mr Campbell would never hurt, let alone kill anybody, so I felt it was my duty to him, and to you, Mrs Campbell, to divert suspicion away from him. I thought you would only be wasting time suspecting him. I am sorry," he repeated, his head in his hands. "What is going to happen to me now?"

McCord was non-committal.

"We'll see," he answered. "First, you'll come down to the station and make a formal statement."

* * *

Proceeding down the mile-long drive with the estate manager following them in the Carnethy Land Rover, McCord made no attempt to contain his glee.

"We've got him, Calderwood, we've got him. Caught in the act, no alibi for the other murders – I reckon we don't even need a motive to satisfy the Lord Advocate."

"In the absence of a confession, I'd be happier if we knew why," Calderwood said. "He just doesn't look like a deranged serial killer to me."

"You sound like our very own Miss Thornton. I'm surprised she didn't turn up at the station first thing this morning trying to persuade us that Andrew Campbell is innocent. I'm sure she has a new theory already."

His phone rang.

"Speak of the devil. It's John Campbell," he said glancing at the display. "They'll be desperate for an update."

He clicked on the green icon.

"DI McCord."

"I am sorry to disturb you during your inquiry." John Campbell's voice with its plummy accent and perfect enunciation had an unusual edge to it.

"No problem," McCord said. "I'm sorry about your brother. What can I do for you?"

"Well, I just wanted to ask if Amy is with you."

"No, she isn't," McCord said, a slight unease creeping up his skin. "I was just saying to DC Calderwood–"

"The point is," John Campbell interrupted McCord with such uncharacteristic rudeness that McCord really began to worry now, "Amy did not turn up for work this morning. At first, I thought she had slept in after the busy day yesterday, but at nine-thirty she was still not here, and she always lets me know if she is late or not coming into the office. When I was unable to reach her on her mobile, I became seriously concerned. She never switches her mobile off, not even at night, so her mum went over to the flat in Queen Street. She is not there, and the bed has not been slept in. I know it usually takes twenty-four hours until the police get involved in a missing person's case, but we were hoping…" His voice trailed off.

McCord cleared his throat where a big lump seemed to have lodged itself, making talking and breathing difficult.

"I'll get onto it as soon as I'm back in town. Meanwhile, ask everybody you can think of if they have heard from her and make a list of places she might have gone." He took a deep breath. "Is it possible that she has a boyfriend she hasn't told anybody about?"

There was a pause while John Campbell considered this possibility.

"I really do not think so," he said eventually.

"Right. Try not to worry. Amy can be a bit of a loose cannon if she gets involved in a case. Maybe she thought she had a lead last night and went off to follow it up. She's a tough cookie, she can look after herself."

"I hope you are right," John Campbell said quietly. "Thank you, DI McCord."

"What's the number of the Queen Street address?"

"67-69."

"Okay. I'll be over as soon as I can."

"Thank you," John Campbell repeated and hung up.

McCord looked at Calderwood, whose face mirrored his own feelings. Without a word, he stepped on the accelerator, forgetting all about the estate manager who was following them into town.

Chapter 16

When Amy woke up, it took her a few moments to remember. She had been kidnapped and thrown into this cold, dark, airless dungeon. But it was no longer completely dark. A thin strip of light indicated the outline of the door she had only felt before. She jumped up, almost tangling herself up in the blankets, and went over to it. She could not see anything through the gap, which was too narrow, but the mere thought of light outside gave her courage. She screamed for help, but soon her voice faltered, and her shouts became moans interrupted by sobs. Shivering with cold, she made her way back to the pile of blankets.

After a while, her tears had dried. She needed to stop panicking and start thinking. She needed to keep her strength up. When had she last eaten? John and her mum had asked her round for a take-away after the removal van had gone, but she had declined. Why on earth had she done that? Then she remembered. Because she was in a strop. She had sensed their concern at her being on her own in a new flat and wanted to prove to them that she was a big girl. If she had joined them, she might never have had that stupid idea of going back to the flat late at night on her own. She would not be here...

'Stop it,' she told herself. There was no point in dwelling on what could have been. She was here now. But what day was this? Monday? Or Tuesday? All she knew was that she was starving. She wriggled out of the blanket, fumbled in the darkness for the parcel and unwrapped it. The ham smelt delicious. She took a large bite of the soft bread. Feeling better already, she put it down and opened the flask. Hot chocolate. Carefully, she poured some into the screw-on cup and took a small sip. It was not too hot, so she drained the makeshift cup in one big gulp. It did not take her long to finish the sandwich and she was about to tear open the bag of crisps when a terrible thought occurred to her. What if Andrew, or whoever the kidnapper was, did not come back? What if he had been killed or was on the run, unable or unwilling to come back and bring her more food or let her go? What if nobody found out that she was here? McCord, she thought, and that immediately calmed her down. McCord would come looking for her, and he and Calderwood would figure out where she was. Just how long would it take? She put down the bag of crisps.

Curled up in her blankets, she stared at the rectangle of light. What if the kidnapper *did* come back, but not in order to bring food or to release her, but to kill her? She had not seen or heard anything that would help her identify him, but did he know that? Maybe he was planning to use her as a bargaining chip, and what if the police did not give in to the blackmail? 'Stop it,' she scolded herself again. She was *not* going to die here. She had to keep her mind busy to stop herself from panicking. She had to figure out what had happened and needed to go back over everything she knew about the four cases. But the only coherent thought that would form in her mind was 'please, McCord, come and get me out of here, please...'

* * *

As soon as they were back at the station and Justin Torrence had been put into an interview room with a guard, McCord called John Campbell. "Any sign of her yet?"

"No, nothing," John said in a compressed voice. "We keep trying to call, but her phone seems to be switched off."

"Does it look as if anybody has broken into the flat?" McCord asked.

"We did not notice anything." John sounded doubtful. "Inside it is rather chaotic, but Amy's belongings had just been dumped by the removal men, so it is difficult to tell."

McCord tried not to let his frustration show. "Have you any idea why she might have gone out?"

"She did not have dinner with us, so she might have gone out to buy some food, but my guess is that she would have ordered a take-away."

Something was tugging at the back of McCord's mind, but he could not get it to take shape.

"Okay. Please don't touch anything for now." He hung up and turned to Calderwood.

"I can't believe Amy's disappearance is a coincidence," McCord said. "Add her details to the incident board and tell Sutton to trace her phone."

He saw Calderwood pulling a face and grinned. "If you're scared of her, send her an email, you coward. Then take Torrence's statement, frighten him a little bit with pending charges and let him go. I'm going to talk to Andrew Campbell, and then to the Super."

Calderwood hesitated.

"Well? What are you waiting for?" McCord asked, impatiently.

"Had I not better be there for the interview with Campbell?"

"No, you hadn't," McCord snapped. "Anyway, it's not a formal interview, I just want to ask him where Amy is. It might save us a lot of time."

"Just…"

"Just what, DC Calderwood?"

"Just remember, sir, we need you on the case, not off it."

"Are you implying that I might act unprofessionally?"

"Even I might if I was alone with Andrew Campbell," Calderwood said.

McCord just snorted and went off. Down at the cells, he gave the duty sergeant, who had just dozed off over a football magazine, the fright of his life.

"The keys to Andrew Campbell's cell, please, once you've finished your beauty sleep. I need to speak to him."

"But… but… should he not have a lawyer present…" the duty sergeant stuttered, fumbling with his keys and eventually finding the correct one.

"No big deal," McCord said and squeezed past the officer into Andrew Campbell's cell. "I just need to ask him something. Go and get us a cup of tea and a biscuit before I set up a disciplinary hearing."

The duty sergeant hurried off.

The prisoner sat up, looking pale and clearly alarmed.

"What's happened?" he asked.

McCord moved towards him, every step a threat.

"What have you done with her?" he asked in his dangerous quiet voice. "Where did you take her?"

"Who? What?" Andrew Campbell stammered.

"Cut the crap," McCord said, his face almost touching the prisoner's. "Where is Amy Thornton?"

"I have no idea," Campbell wailed, backing against the wall, "why would I know?"

"Did she find out what you were up to, and you had to get rid of her? Did you kill her as well?"

"No, I didn't!" Campbell shrieked. "And I haven't killed anybody! Are you trying to pin every crime in the city on me? I have no idea where she is!"

His eyes widened in terror, and McCord thought of what Mr Cooper would make of the intimidation of suspects.

Behind him, the duty sergeant cleared his throat.

"Sir," he started timidly. "Here is the tea and the biscuits you asked for. I was on night shift three times this week, you know… I'm sorry, it won't happen again."

"Okay, okay." McCord had returned to his normal voice. "Mr Campbell is a bit on edge after a night in the cells. Give him a cup of tea and a biscuit, and your job is on the line if you ever fall asleep again while on duty!"

On his way back to the office, he knocked on Superintendent Gilchrist's door. He was only too happy to see McCord.

"Four murders now on your patch! Four!" he thundered. "And Andrew Campbell arrested?"

"When the officers arrived at the scene after being called out to a suspected burglary, Campbell was found kneeling next to Buchan's body. His alibis for two of the murders have collapsed."

"Indeed, so why has it taken you so long to nail him down?"

McCord was speechless for a moment but then remembered why he was here.

"I need you to authorise a full-scale search for a missing person. Amy Thornton has disappeared."

"Amy Thornton? The journalist who helped us with the McAdie case?"

"The very same," McCord said. "She has not turned up for work, nor been in touch with her family."

Gilchrist looked doubtful.

"I suppose now that we've caught the killer, we can spare the manpower. How long has she been missing?"

"Since last night, possibly," McCord said, his stomach churning. "I am wondering if her disappearance is connected to the murders. It seems too much of a coincidence."

"Maybe, but a bit early for a full-scale call-out," the Super decided. "Let's wait until tomorrow morning. That way we follow regulations and don't look like complete prats if she turns up with a hangover after a couple of boozy nights with a new boyfriend."

Having prepared himself for that argument, McCord played his ace.

"I'm not sure you are aware that John Campbell has just moved in with Amy's mother, which makes Amy de facto his stepdaughter. Mr Campbell has been on the phone several times; he is most anxious to find her. And his mother, Mrs Edith Campbell, will not be happy if she hears that her son's future stepdaughter's disappearance has not been investigated immediately. She is not best pleased with the situation as it is."

He had been right. Gilchrist's concerns melted away.

"Good point, McCord, good point. Make sure you find her and please be quicker about it than you have been with all these murders."

With such encouraging words ringing in his ears, McCord returned to his office. Calderwood, who had just come back from his interview with Torrence, looked at McCord's fists as if he expected them to be caked in blood.

"Anything?" Calderwood asked.

"Andrew Campbell denies abducting Amy but who knows? He is a habitual liar, after all. But on the way down it occurred to me that he would have had to attack – kidnap, whatever – Amy before he murdered Buchan. But why would he do that? Did she find out something, and rather than tell us, decide to talk to him first? Did he then realise that she knew too much and…"

He did not finish the sentence. Calderwood knew what he meant.

"What did the Super say?"

"He agrees with me for once. Send a forensics team out to 67-69 Queen Street to look for signs of forced entry or a struggle. I want DC Sutton to get into Amy's laptop and her credit card transactions. Get Amy's picture from the magazine articles, organise a door-to-door in Queen Street, as well as the nearest side streets, and check all grocery shops and take-aways in the neighbourhood. Got that?"

"Got it," Calderwood said.

* * *

Outside the Queen Street flat, McCord found Valerie pacing up and down like one of the neurotic big cats sometimes seen in a zoo. There was no point in asking if there had been any news.

"Are you okay?" he inquired, knowing this was an equally stupid question but one that was customary, to show that one cared.

Valerie stopped in front of him, her long, auburn hair a mess, her beautiful face distorted with fear.

"DI McCord, where is she?"

"We'll find her."

How he managed to sound confident, he did not know. He examined the lock and the doorframe carefully but could detect no sign of forced entry.

Just then John arrived, carrying a tray of coffees and a paper bag bulging with snacks.

"I thought we could all do with some sustenance," he explained. "Valerie has not been able to eat anything this morning, have you, dear."

McCord gratefully sipped a flat white and bit into a chocolate muffin, while John was trying to coax Valerie into having at least a muesli bar.

"Forensics and the other officers should be here any minute," McCord said. "By now, every police officer in the city will be looking for her."

"Do you think it was Andrew?" John Campbell asked quietly.

"If he did," Valerie butted in, "he would be interrogating him and making him tell us where she is, wouldn't you?" She turned to McCord. "Wouldn't you?" she repeated.

"I *have* spoken to him," McCord said, trying to sound neutral. "He denies all knowledge."

"But he would, wouldn't he?" Valerie insisted. "No, John" – she waved away his objections – "you need to face the fact that he is a killer. And now he has taken my girl!"

She began to sob uncontrollably.

McCord tried to calm her down. "We don't know that. Do you have any idea why Alexander Buchan was at your shop last night at 9pm? I thought the flat had been sold."

But Valerie was caught in a maelstrom of despair and not able to think straight, so John answered for her.

"The buyer kept delaying the entry date, and we were worried that he might pull out altogether, but Mr Buchan had found a second one who was interested. Maybe he was showing them around?"

"At that time of day?" McCord wondered.

"He once complained about the anti-social hours he has to do. They have to accommodate their clients if they want to view properties before or after work."

McCord nodded, making a mental note to check with the estate agency who the potential buyers were.

"Look," he said, pointing to the line of vans and police cars approaching, "here comes the cavalry."

Chapter 17

"I've been thinking about a motive for all the murders," Calderwood said when McCord arrived back at the station. He hesitated.

"And?" McCord asked expectantly.

"You won't like it."

"Why wouldn't I? So far, there has been a distinct lack of ideas regarding the motive."

"I was asking myself who benefits most from the current situation."

"And?" McCord repeated, growing impatient.

"John Campbell."

"What?" McCord blurted out. "Rubbish!"

"Where do we look first when a crime is committed?" Calderwood said. "The family. With Andrew out of the way, John Campbell is on course to inherit the whole estate. Why is he not there anyway? Why does he live in a flat in George Street running a niche magazine?"

"I'm not sure," McCord replied. "Amy never talked about that. I assumed it was because of his mother, and Andrew – they don't get on very well…"

Calderwood shook his head at the word 'assumed', and McCord had to admit that John had never occurred to him as a potential suspect.

"With his brother going down for four brutal murders," Calderwood pressed on, "his magazine, which was not exactly a goldmine until the McAdie case, will be selling like hotcakes again."

"Rubbish," McCord said again, but less emphatically.

"All the evidence we have against Andrew Campbell is circumstantial. Maybe he has been framed for all the murders. John Campbell knows what brand his brother smokes, he has access to the rocks, he could have written the *A* next to Walker's body to draw our attention to Andrew… does he have an alibi for the times of the murders?"

"I have no idea," McCord admitted.

"There you are," Calderwood concluded. "I'll get onto that, shall I?"

Four brutal murders, McCord thought, and sending his own brother to prison for life to inherit a multi-million-pound estate? No, surely not. It couldn't be. Could it? Calderwood was right. He had been sloppy in his investigation. He had been guided by feelings rather than procedure. And why? Because Amy loved John like a father, and this possibility would hurt her beyond words. And, he admitted grudgingly to himself because, apart from Calderwood, John was the only toff he had ever come across that he liked.

A ping on his phone jolted him out of his gloomy thoughts: a message from DC Sutton.

> *No trace of the phone after 7pm last night, no credit card movements.*

He rang the DS supervising the door-to-door enquiries.

"Anything?"

"Nothing yet, sir. People saw the removal van arrive and leave, but nothing afterwards."

"Thanks. Keep looking."

The office phone shrilled. It was the duty sergeant at the main entrance.

"There's someone here to see you about Amy Thornton, sir."

His heart leapt.

"Send them up."

He and Calderwood looked at each other hopefully. A possible witness?

The man fluttering into the office did not, at first glance, give the impression of somebody one would want to put on a witness stand. The inspiration for his outfit had clearly come from Elvis's legendary white rhinestone suit, only there was not a spot of boring white on this one, which was a riot of primary colours.

"DI McCord, I presume?" the visitor twittered. "I have heard so much about you. *So* sorry to disturb you but I just *had* to pop in."

"And you are?" McCord asked, wondering if he had dozed off and landed in a bizarre dream.

"I *do* apologise. I have not been able to think straight since our dearest Amy disappeared. Martin Eden, subeditor of *Forth Write* magazine."

A bird of paradise, right enough.

"Pleased to meet you, Mr Eden," McCord said, now all ears. "Do you have any information that might help us find her?"

"Not as *such*," Martin said. "But I wanted to be sure that you take her disappearance seriously. John, I mean Mr Campbell, the owner, is always so polite and... measured that I was worried that you did not appreciate how *desperate* the situation is."

McCord sighed inwardly.

"I can assure you, Mr Eden, that we are taking Miss Thornton's disappearance very seriously. I have already launched a full-scale search."

Martin spread his arms as if to embrace everybody in the office.

"*Thank* you. I know that Amy thinks the world of you even if she does not always express it. She's very independent, you know."

McCord did not comment. He just cleared his throat, wondering how he could get rid of this strange bird, but then he had a thought. "Have you known Amy and John Campbell long?" he asked conversationally.

"Well, Amy since she joined the magazine four years ago. John I've known *forever*; we were at uni together."

"Have you noticed a change in John Campbell recently?"

"A change?" Martin's eyes narrowed. "What do you mean, 'change'?"

He is not stupid, this one, McCord decided, despite the ridiculous outfit.

"I mean his mood, his demeanour, different habits?"

"John is not somebody who wears his heart on his sleeve," Martin said, suddenly guarded. "But he has certainly been a happier man since he met Valerie. He simply *adores* her – *and* Amy," he added pointedly.

"That's the impression I have as well," McCord said. "Thank you for coming in, Mr Eden. Let me know if you can think of anything at all that might help us find Miss Thornton."

* * *

When Martin had taken off, McCord leant back in his chair, his fingertips touching.

"See?" he said to Calderwood. "Everyone likes John Campbell."

"Everyone liked Jimmy Savile," Calderwood retorted. "I still believe, and so do you, that Amy's disappearance is linked to the murders. That leads us back to the Campbells. If Amy let somebody into the flat, it is likely to be someone she knew and trusted. Back to the Campbells. And where would either of the Campbells hide the–" Calderwood could not bring himself to say 'body' "–someone? In an area spreading across hundreds of acres where they know every nook and cranny. On their estate."

McCord scratched his chin, looking grim. "Come on," he told Calderwood. "We're going up to Carnethy."

"Should we not interview John Campbell first?"

"I'd rather he didn't realise that we suspect him yet. Let's go."

* * *

It was getting close to lunchtime as they wound their way up the Carnethy Estate drive for the second time that day. McCord had been debating with himself if he should have ordered a search party straightaway, but he was hoping that Mrs Campbell would be more co-operative without helicopters of police circling overhead. Once he made the call, the search party would be here within the hour, and if Amy was still alive, and she simply *had* to be, it would not make a difference.

As they approached the house, it was obvious that they were by no means the only people trying to speak to Mrs Campbell. The media circus had already arrived.

Photographers were taking pictures of the front of the mansion; most hacks hovered by the main entrance, while others tried their luck at the side doors.

The Juke crunched to a halt in the third row of vehicles parked in front of the stone steps. McCord and Calderwood had to push their way through the crowd up to the door. When they got there, McCord hesitated. He hated facing a mob, and the last time he had spoken to the media, he was lambasted later by the Super for his pains. Then he noticed that one enterprising group of paparazzi had brought a ladder and were trying to take pictures through a first-floor window.

"Right," McCord said to himself.

He turned round and held up his ID.

"Police!" he shouted.

There was an immediate hush in the crowd, and over a hundred expectant eyes were on McCord. He took a deep breath.

"You are all trespassing on private property and interfering with a police investigation. I am ordering you to leave immediately."

Grumbling, the reporters returned to their vehicles, and after a few minutes, a long line of traffic snaked back to the front gates.

"Nicely done," Calderwood said. "That should put you in Mrs Campbell's good books."

McCord pressed the bell. The melodious gong echoed inside, but it took another three attempts until they heard somebody approaching the door.

"Go away!" they heard Edith Campbell's imperious voice through the door. "We shall not be giving any interviews. If you don't leave, I shall call the police!"

"DI McCord and DC Calderwood," McCord shouted through the door. "Please let us in."

After a brief wait, the door was unlocked and opened. Edith Campbell looked at them, mildly disgusted.

"I thought you were press," Edith Campbell said, but her voice made it clear that they were not much more welcome. She looked around.

"They've gone," she commented, and appraised McCord with a look now decidedly above freezing. "Come in."

"We are sorry to disturb you, ma'am," Calderwood began, only to be interrupted by McCord.

"We have reason to believe that a young woman, Amy Thornton, has been kidnapped and is possibly held here on the estate."

"Kidnapped? Here on the estate?" Edith Campbell repeated, aghast. "Amy Thornton, the journalist who was here before with my son, John?" Edith Campbell asked. "Why on earth would she be here on our estate?"

Calderwood's voice was calm itself. "We are not entirely sure that she *is* here, but we thought it better to check discreetly first. A full-scale search for Miss Thornton has been launched in the city, and if we find her quickly, it might not be necessary to send search parties and helicopters onto the estate."

"Search parties? Helicopters?" Edith Campbell whispered in horror.

"Do you have any idea where she could be hidden if she is on the estate?" Calderwood asked.

Edith Campbell still resisted the mere suggestion that her estate could be the scene of a kidnap.

"What about the house?" Calderwood suggested. "There must be dozens of rooms."

"Fifty-seven," Edith Campbell corrected automatically. "But I doubt very much that she is here. As a matter of fact, Lucy went round all the rooms this morning to check that everything is in order."

"I think I'd rather have a look myself," McCord said.

"Most estates have a few derelict buildings," Calderwood suggested. "Why don't we check them out? We'll need some torches as well, for any dark places where there is no power. Maybe your estate manager could guide us."

"He is somewhere out on the estate. After his ordeal this morning," she said pointedly, "I gave him the rest of the day off, but he said he would just carry on."

"Well, can't you show us round?" McCord demanded, losing his patience.

With an exasperated sigh, Edith Campbell rose.

"I think this is completely mad. But I suppose…"

"Lead the way," McCord said. "First the house, then the grounds."

* * *

After stumbling over roots, stubbing his toes on stones and squelching through mud for the best part of an hour, McCord's optimism had waned. Amy was not in the house, and after searching that, they had peered into deserted stables, old tool sheds and mothballed staff accommodation, and all in vain. What if he had been wrong? What if they were wasting valuable time here when the answer lay elsewhere, as the lawyer had suggested? What if her body was buried somewhere on a moor, never to be recovered? The answer was simple; he was desperate to do *something*, anything that might help find Amy.

Suddenly, Edith Campbell stopped in her tracks, almost causing McCord to bump into her from behind.

"The old icehouse!" she exclaimed. "That would be a perfect place to hide somebody! Why didn't I think of that before? Andrew used to go down there when he was small to hide from invading aliens."

She turned off down a track to the right, and soon they all approached a stony mound covered in moss and grasses. Edith Campbell struggled to lift the latch, and Calderwood rushed forward to assist her. McCord hung back, suddenly dreading what they might find. The heavy door creaked open, and Calderwood bent down to get inside.

"Amy? Are you there? She's here! She's alive!" he shouted back to them.

A strange sound escaped McCord, which he quickly covered with a cough. Blinking into the flickering autumn light, Amy emerged from her prison, looking dazed and with her arms wrapped around herself against the cold.

"Are you okay, Amy?" Calderwood hovered over her to examine her more closely. "Are you hurt?"

"I'm fine," she said, looking at McCord, who was ghastly pale. "You're clearly feeling a lot worse than I am."

There was an awkward moment when all Amy wanted was to hug McCord, but Calderwood took her by the arm, ostensibly to support her.

McCord had regained some of his colour. "Sorry, it took us so long to find you."

Amy shivered. "I was beginning to think I might die in there."

"Let's get her back to the house to get warm," Edith Campbell suggested sensibly.

"And then you need to tell us everything that happened," Calderwood said, while McCord pulled out his phone.

"We've found her," McCord informed his colleagues at the station. "Call off the search."

He stood for a moment, staring at his phone. Then he dialled another number.

The person he called picked up on the first ring.

"We've found her. She is fine," McCord said.

There was a moment's silence at the other end, then a torrent of praise and gratitude. He listened impatiently; then he cut the call.

"Who was that?" Amy asked curiously.

"John Campbell," he offered reluctantly and exchanged a glance with Calderwood, who looked at him, frowning.

"How does he know?" Amy asked.

"He and your mum were worried when you didn't turn up at work. When they checked the flat and couldn't get you on your phone, they realised you had disappeared, so he called me."

Amy sighed. "He is just the best."

McCord said nothing.

Amy being Amy found it quite impossible to wait with her tale until they were at the house. She described in detail why and how she had entered the shop but hesitated at the description of the bulky object on the floor.

"Was that...?" she asked McCord.

"Alexander Buchan," he confirmed. "Same MO as the others. The police got a tip-off about a burglary at the shop, and when they arrived, they found Andrew Campbell there with the body."

"Oh my God," Amy exclaimed. "How awful. I'm so sorry, Mrs Campbell," she added. "I can't believe it. Poor John!"

"Did you notice anything about the kidnapper?" McCord asked. "Height, voice, anything?"

Amy shook her head.

"They pressed a funny-smelling cloth over my mouth and nose, and I lost consciousness almost immediately. When I woke up, it was pitch dark and freezing cold. Thank God, he had left me a couple of blankets and some food. I saw or heard nothing until Duncan called out my name at the door."

* * *

Having brushed down his jacket and trousers, McCord lowered himself into an armchair and watched Amy sip a coffee laced with cognac. Edith Campbell had offered something stronger from the drink cabinet, anything but the twenty-year-old Laphroaig, which was Andrew's. This, she added with a side glance to McCord, would be waiting for him to celebrate his release from jail. McCord stuck to plain coffee and savoured the delicious feeling that Amy was safe and well and that he had played a not inconsiderable part in her rescue.

On their way back, McCord wondered how he could keep Amy away from the Campbells without arousing suspicion.

"I'll drop DC Calderwood off at the station, and then I'll take you home so that you can have a shower and get changed," McCord said. "Your mum will be desperate to see you, too. Then we'll get you something to eat on the way to the station. We need an official statement from you and I would like to bounce a few ideas off you."

Calderwood looked like thunder, and Amy shot a sideways glance at McCord.

"Are you feeling quite well?" she asked.

Chapter 18

Valerie hugged her daughter so hard that Amy winced.

"I don't know what I would have done if..." she began. As she kissed Amy's head, she looked across to McCord. "I don't know how to thank you for finding her."

Eventually, Amy wriggled free.

"I really need a shower," she announced, "and I'm starving."

They went upstairs. Forensics had left after being told that the flat was no longer considered a potential crime scene. The place was chaotic. A feeble attempt had been made to label some of the boxes and binbags, but Amy tore open five of them before locating her toiletries and some clothes suitable for a chilly October day. McCord listened to the running shower, and picturing Amy in there fogged his brain for a moment. But then he dragged himself back to reality. He needed to keep her safe. He had to catch that killer.

"Did Mr Campbell go out last night?" he asked as casually as he could. "It's just I thought I saw him in town across the street."

Valerie shook her head.

"No, we were very tired after the move last night. We had a Chinese take-away and a bottle of wine and just collapsed in bed. I must have been asleep by eight."

"I'm sure there is still a lot to do to set up the new shop," McCord said before Valerie had a chance to wonder why he was interested in John's whereabouts.

"Of course, I couldn't think of anything else while Amy was missing," Valerie said. "I haven't even unpacked my sewing machine yet!"

"Why don't you get on with your work," McCord suggested. "Amy needs to come to the station asap anyway to make a statement, and I'll make sure she gets something to eat."

Valerie hesitated. "John will be upset he missed her, but maybe we can take her out for dinner later."

McCord did not let on how much he disliked the idea, but he could not think of a reason why they should not.

"I'll tell her to call you later," McCord promised.

"She is not still in danger, is she?" Valerie suddenly asked. She saw McCord's hesitation, even if it lasted only a split second. "You think she is, don't you? Why would you be here otherwise?"

"I'm not sure," he said honestly. "There are aspects of the case that just don't make sense. And until they do, I'll do my damnedest to make sure Amy is safe."

Valerie gave him a spontaneous hug.

"I know, DI McCord. I know."

* * *

When Valerie had gone, McCord pulled out his phone and called Calderwood.

"I want a tail on John Campbell, 124 George Street," he whispered. "Yes, 24/7. If he so much as coughs, I want to know about it."

* * *

"Feeling better?" McCord asked when Amy came out of the bathroom dressed for business in a dark trouser suit and a pink polo neck, towelling her long, dark hair.

"A lot better. I need to iron my blouses first," she explained, misreading his slightly pained expression.

"You always look great," he said stiffly.

Amy wrapped the towel skilfully into a turban and moved closer until she stood right in front of him. A drop of water escaped from her hair and ran down her neck.

"I haven't really thanked you yet. You probably saved my life," she said, suddenly serious.

Tentatively, she held out her arms, and when he did not recoil, she embraced him and planted a lingering kiss on his cheek. Too stunned to move, he found himself released before he could hug her back.

Amy started rummaging through boxes for her hairdryer and eventually spotted the cable.

"Your mum and John want to take you out for dinner tonight," McCord said. "I told her you'd phone to make arrangements."

"Will do, thanks. It was very considerate of the kidnapper to leave me my phone. He must have known there was no reception in the icehouse. It looks as if he just wanted me out of the way but tried hard not to hurt me."

"I agree," McCord shouted over the noise of the hairdryer, hoping she would make the logical leap to John Campbell, but she said nothing more until her hair was dry and brushed into a neat ponytail.

"It's already three o'clock. If I'm eating out tonight, I can just pick up a snack on the way. As long as it's not a ham sandwich."

* * *

When they arrived back at the station later in the afternoon, Calderwood cornered McCord in the men's toilets.

"Why did you tell John Campbell straight away that we had found her? He might be plotting another attempt as we speak!"

McCord calmly continued to dry his hands.

"*He* reported her missing, remember?"

"A ploy to divert suspicion," Calderwood declared.

"Listen. Firstly, Amy's mother needed to know anyway. Secondly, if he is behind this, we don't want to let on that we know."

"And how are we going to protect her from him if she trusts him implicitly? You can't keep her here overnight, or is that what you're aiming at?"

"Careful now," McCord said. "We just have to try. John Campbell is being tailed day and night. Andrew is safely out of the way. In the meantime, we need to check John's whereabouts for the times of the murders, but discreetly. If he turns out to be innocent and we destroy Amy's trust in him, she'll never forgive us."

* * *

In the office, Amy was writing her meagre witness statement at McCord's desk. When she reached the part where she had entered the shop, she lowered her pen.

"It doesn't make any sense," she said, more to herself than anybody in the room. "Duncan, could I see the photos from the crime scene, please?"

Calderwood hesitated.

"I don't think those pictures are something a lady should see," he ventured. "You would never forget them, and you might end up having nightmares."

Amy bristled but McCord beat her to a reply.

"She's seen worse in real life; she can cope," he said drily. "Just bring them over."

Calderwood got up and placed the file in front of Amy, looking over her shoulder. Not to be outdone, McCord also took position behind her, catching the slightest hint of a fragrance, fresh, fruity with a sharpness around the edges. With difficulty he resisted the temptation to lean closer, to breathe it in more deeply.

"What is it?" he asked quietly, thinking of both the fragrance and the picture.

"That is what I saw," Amy said. "When I entered the shop, I saw Buchan's body lying there."

The detectives didn't answer; neither of them pointed out that this was not exactly news.

"But don't you see?" Amy grew exasperated. "You are so slow on the uptake. If Andrew killed Buchan *and* kidnapped me, he would have to have killed him, driven me the best part of half an hour up to the estate, organised the blanket and the food and then driven back to be arrested next to the body. Does that make sense to either of you?"

She turned round, causing both men to quickly retreat.

"It doesn't," McCord admitted, wondering how long they could keep their suspicion of John Campbell from her.

"Maybe Buchan was not dead when you saw him," Calderwood suggested. "Maybe he was only knocked out. You surprised Andrew Campbell, he had to get rid of you, and then he returned to finish Buchan off."

Neither McCord nor Amy dignified this theory with an answer.

"And something else doesn't make sense," Amy said, continuing her train of thought. "The report says that the lights were on when the police arrived. If you wanted to kill somebody, would you do it with the lights on, so that everybody passing the place in the street could see what you were doing?" She shook her head, giving the answer herself. "When I went into the shop, the lights were switched off at the mains. I must have come in just seconds after the murder, and it only makes sense for the killer to kidnap me."

She shuddered at the memory.

"But then why the estate?" Calderwood interjected. "Hiding you on the estate only makes sense if it was Andrew Campbell or–"

McCord shot him a warning look, shook his head and said, "It looks to me as if somebody has deliberately tried to frame Andrew Campbell for the murders from the beginning. The cigarette stub, the rocks, the *A* painted in blood... Dr Crane had said it was surprising that Walker was able to write a message after the attack – well, maybe he didn't. I think it was the killer trying to point us in Andrew Campbell's direction. And I was such a moron, I fell for it. So, it makes sense for the killer to hide you somewhere on the estate to incriminate Andrew further. The papers were full of his circumstances and of him living on a large estate; it was the obvious place: huge, sprawling and hardly anybody about."

McCord paced up and down the office.

"Damn – I mean, I'm pleased that it looks like John's brother is not a murderer," McCord corrected himself hastily, looking at Amy. "But I'd rather postpone his release until we know more, just in case we are wrong. The twenty-four hours are not up yet, and his lawyer will be in soon enough. Amy, we need your help. In order to find out who is behind this, we need to establish a motive. Why don't you research the time the group was at university? Old newspaper reports, social media, YouTube, whatever..."

Amy was ecstatic at last to be a proper part of the investigation.

"I'm on it!"

* * *

After convincing the Super that it was necessary to keep a close eye on Amy Thornton, McCord had requisitioned her from the magazine, and John Campbell had not objected, even if he did not sound pleased.

"As long as she has her article ready in time for the weekend edition," he said.

McCord assured him that she would, and that with Andrew's expected release and the hunt for the real killer continuing, the story would be even more sensational than before.

The officers following John Campbell reported no suspicious activity. He had spent most of his time at the magazine or in his flat upstairs, and in the afternoon, he had helped Valerie in her new premises in Queen Street.

Knowing that Amy was safe, McCord was able to concentrate on the case itself once more. He phoned Buchan's estate agency and asked the secretary to find details about the potential buyers of Valerie Thornton's flat and shop. The young woman was pleased to help.

"Ms Thornton has had an offer from a Mr Craig Higginbottom," she said, and reeled off the address and phone number, "but then he seemed to have second thoughts and asked for a delay of the money transfer. Mr Buchan was *not* happy, as you can imagine. But then, almost immediately, somebody else showed an interest."

"What was his name and address?" McCord asked when there was a moment's silence on the phone.

"That's odd," the secretary said. "The file is incomplete. It just says James Brown, and a phone number, to be dealt with by Mr Buchan only."

"Very interesting," McCord said while jotting the number down. "Thank you."

He went over to Sutton's workstation and handed her a Post-it note with the number. "DC Sutton, this number could lead us to the killer," he explained, "I need it traced quickly."

DC Sutton did not look up from her screen, and he wondered if she had heard him.

"Email from Robert McArthur to his friends seven years ago."

She clicked a key, and the whining sound of a sheet of paper being squeezed out of the printer filled the small space. She handed McCord the printout, took the Post-it note and resumed work.

McCord scanned the email and hurried back to office. Seeing that Amy was engrossed in her internet searches, he motioned to Calderwood to meet him in the corridor.

"Look at this: Sutton has just given me this email from Robbie McArthur to Jordan Lamond, Zac Walker and Andrew Campbell asking them to help him convince Cheryl to get rid of the baby because the maintenance would ruin him."

Calderwood whistled softly through his teeth.

"So, Cheryl Gibbs didn't want to have an abortion initially. That would fit in with her Catholic background. Do you think 'The Players' put pressure on her somehow?"

McCord picked up his jacket.

"Come on, we need to speak to William and Cheryl Gibbs now."

* * *

The couple were none too pleased about another visit from DI McCord.

"What do you want this time?" William Gibbs demanded angrily. "We've told you everything in our statement. You're upsetting my wife, and she is not well."

"New evidence has come to light, and we need to hear what you have to say. And that includes your wife."

The bedroom door opened, and Cheryl Gibbs, wrapped in an oversized bathrobe, shuffled in.

"Hello, Mrs Gibbs."

McCord assumed that she had been listening through the door, so he did not bother repeating what he had said.

"What new evidence?" Gibbs asked, less aggressive and more worried now.

"It seems that seven years ago Robert McArthur enlisted the help of his friends to put pressure on you, Mrs Gibbs, to have an abortion. Is that correct?"

Mrs Gibbs burst into tears, and her husband's resigned expression told McCord that he knew denial was futile.

"Yes, they did, the bastards," Gibbs said. "Robert McArthur was not willing to face up to his responsibilities. They threatened Cheryl with spreading lies about her alleged promiscuous lifestyle and making it known to her parents that she had slept with all of them. Andrew Campbell also had connections to the

Head of Faculty; that's how he got onto his course in the first place, thickhead that he is. He told Cheryl that she could forget her degree if she didn't play ball. In the end, she was so frightened and disgusted with Robbie that she went along with it."

"I am sorry," McCord said truthfully. "And why did you call Zacharias Walker two days before his death?"

Gibbs turned pale.

"How…? I suppose you lot can get at all our data now just like that. I called him to say that I was glad that somebody had done Robert McArthur in and that I hoped that he would get his comeuppance as well. But I didn't kill them!"

McCord remained unmoved.

"I'm afraid I must ask you to come to the station for a formal interview under caution. You might want to take a few things – this could take a long time."

Gibbs looked at him, scared.

"Please, we… you can't…"

Mrs Gibbs started to sob hysterically.

"Please," Gibbs pleaded, "Cheryl…"

McCord's jaw had set.

"You can arrange for a family member or friend to look after her before we go," McCord suggested. "I need to make a call."

He went into the hall and dialled DC Sutton's number.

"Look for a connection of the phone number I gave you with William or Cheryl Gibbs. Thanks."

* * *

Back at the station, Gibbs, perhaps unsurprisingly, had a clear recollection of where he was during the times of the murders. When Robert McArthur was killed, he said, repeating his earlier statement, he was on his way to Birmingham for a conference, but in Zacharias Walker's and Alex Buchan's case, he claimed to have been at home with his wife. Calderwood took a DNA sample from him, and after telling him not to leave town, McCord released him.

After he had left, McCord was uncharacteristically subdued.

"You don't want it to be him, do you?" Calderwood ventured to ask.

"Not really," McCord admitted. "But what bugs me is the murder of Alexander Buchan. He was not included in the email and, being in love with Cheryl Langley, he would have tried to protect her, one would have thought. So, why kill him?"

"Maybe he was a right coward and did nothing in the end so as not to upset his 'friends'. With their connections, they could have done him damage if he had turned against them. Or perhaps" – Calderwood's eyes lit up – "Buchan figured out that Gibbs was the killer and threatened to expose him. Remember, Andrew Campbell said he got a message from Buchan telling him he knew who the murderer was. Maybe that was it, and when Andrew arrived at the scene, he stumbled upon the body, just like he said."

Chapter 19

Just before tea time, Amy looked up from her screen.

"What is it?" McCord asked, seeing she was clearly shocked.

"I think I might have found a motive for all the murders," she said quietly, but there was no glee in her voice.

"You have?" Calderwood blurted out. After all, they knew about John Campbell's and William Gibbs' motive, didn't they?

"Let's see then," McCord said, pulling up a chair next to her as she clicked on a link on YouTube.

Calderwood, not wanting to miss out, sidled over as well.

"I was looking at posts from thirteen years ago that had a connection with Edinburgh University or Andrew Campbell and his friends, and I found this. It was posted under the title *Royal Blush* by people calling themselves 'The Players'."

Obviously filmed with a webcam, the grainy, black-and-white video showed a small room with six men around a table, playing cards. McCord and Calderwood recognised Zacharias Walker and Alexander Buchan, just slightly younger and slimmer versions of themselves, and the towering figure to their right was Robbie McArthur. Facing the camera but clearly unaware of it was a lanky young man, stripped to the waist, showing his white, hairless chest, looking distressed. Two men were sitting with their backs to the camera, but when one of them spoke, there was no doubt that it was Andrew Campbell's arrogant drawl.

"Come on, Kevin, you're not going to chicken out now, are you? You are such a great player – your luck is bound to turn!"

The man called Kevin, clearly torn between the desire to run away and to impress the others, stared at the cards in his hand. Then, suddenly making up his mind, he pushed all his remaining notes and coins towards the middle of the table with the others cheering him on.

Andrew Campbell equalled the stakes. Then he leant back in his seat.

"Let's see your hand then," he demanded, with only a quiver of anticipation in his voice.

The half-naked man slowly fanned out the cards.

"A straight," he said.

"Brilliant," Andrew Campbell said appreciatively, and relief flooded the other man's face.

"But that doesn't beat a royal flush."

He held up his hand, so that the camera caught the five spades, and then lowered them onto the table with a flourish.

"That is three grand for me."

The others roared with laughter but there was no surprise in their reaction.

"It was a set up," McCord observed. "Bastards."

The man called Kevin looked at each of them in horror.

"Please, please, I can't…"

"That's the rules of the game, Kevin boy," Andrew Campbell said, his voice as hard as steel now.

"Pants off, pants off, pants off," chanted the others.

Kevin made to flee but realising he would have to leave the room in his underpants, hesitated a moment too long. Robbie McArthur lifted him up like a doll, as Zac Walker and Alex Buchan pulled his boxer shorts down, the camera revealing a shrunken penis between pale, spindly legs.

"There's a sight for sore eyes," Andrew Campbell laughed. "You still think you can be one of us? But we don't want to be too harsh. Robbie, give him his clothes back, so he can crawl back into whatever hole he came from."

Robbie tossed them onto the floor, grinning. Kevin scrambled to pick up his underpants, got his leg stuck and fell over. The others howled with laughter. Eventually, Kevin managed to get his trousers and shirt on and fled the room. The occupants toasted Andrew Campbell's win to the sound of Tom Jones's *You can leave your hat on*, and then the video was cut.

Nobody spoke for a full minute.

"Could this be it?" McCord broke the silence. "Could this Kevin have killed them all? Is he framing Andrew Campbell? The ultimate revenge on the leader of the pack; to spend the rest of his life in prison, humiliated and disgraced?"

They all looked at the last still of the video.

"If this Kevin is the killer," Calderwood said fiercely, "I almost sympathise with him. Those utter swines."

"Well done, Amy," McCord said. "Calderwood, get DC Sutton onto it, and find us this Kevin, asap."

Seeing the look on Calderwood's face, he sighed.

"Okay, I'll ask her myself."

* * *

DC Sutton had constructed yet another obstacle against intruders into her workspace by wheeling a couple of man-sized filing cabinets at right angles to the partition separating her from the outside world. McCord knocked gently on the outer cabinet.

"DC Sutton? May I come in?"

Having received an affirmative answer, he weaved his way towards her but stopped as far away from her as possible.

"Everything okay?" he asked, pointing to the reinforcements.

"People just keep barging in," she complained.

McCord waited a moment for her to elaborate but, of course, she did not.

"DC Sutton, I need your help. We need to find a guy called Kevin who was at university with Andrew Campbell and his friends. DC Calderwood is going to email you a picture and the relevant dates."

"I'm still working on that phone number," she objected. "Not finished yet."

"I am sorry, but this is more important now. This Kevin could be the killer, and as long as he is free, other people might be in danger. We need to know who and where he is, as quickly as possible."

DC Sutton sighed and turned back to her computer.

* * *

Later in the evening, it was time to let Andrew Campbell go.

"I knew you would get there in the end," Alan Cooper said as he shook hands with McCord. "I take it you have another lead?"

"We do," McCord said. "Three in fact. But," he said, turning to Andrew Campbell who had lost some of his flamboyance after a night in a cell, "this investigation is not finished yet. Please don't leave Edinburgh or the estate without telling us."

"It is finished as far as I'm concerned," Andrew Campbell said. "You just don't want to admit that you got it wrong."

"If you had answered my questions truthfully, I would have got there more quickly," McCord shot back, suppressing the desire to punch him. "Does the name Kevin Jones mean anything to you?"

Andrew Campbell screwed up his face trying to remember.

"Kevin Jones, Kevin Jones – wasn't there someone of that name in my year at uni?"

"Well done," McCord praised him sarcastically. "Do you also remember what happened at the last poker game you had with him before he dropped out?"

A grin spread across Andrew Campbell's face.

"Yes, it's coming back to me now. He lost at strip poker. Pathetic guy, always trying to get in with us. Clung on like a limpet, so we had to do something to put him in his place. We let him win a few times at poker until he fancied himself as a great player, and then we taught him a lesson."

"And what a lesson it was," McCord continued. "He has certainly never forgotten it. We have reason to believe that he has killed the other four from your group, and if I had to make a wager, I'd put money on him coming after you now."

"Kevin Jones?" Andrew Campbell laughed. "No way. He was so wet; he wouldn't say boo to a goose."

"Well, whoever the killer is, he has eliminated four out of the five of you. If I were the fifth person, I'd be looking over my shoulder."

Andrew Campbell stopped laughing. "You really think it was Kevin Jones?"

"I have no proof yet," McCord replied, "but it is a distinct possibility. Mr Cooper, maybe you can encourage your client to take the matter a little more seriously?"

"I'll try," the lawyer replied. "Come on, Andrew, your mother is waiting outside on a double yellow line to take you home."

"I thought John was coming to pick me up?" Andrew asked.

"He's out of town today; he's going to join you later. Hurry up, she can't wait to see you."

McCord watched them going down the corridor, pulled out his phone and made a call.

"Why didn't anybody tell me that John Campbell is out of town?" he said in his dangerous quiet voice. "Where the hell is he?"

"Sorry, sir. He's been tailed to Glasgow," the DC at the other end said.

McCord grunted.

"Let me know as soon as he's on his way back."

* * *

"Nice to see you, Russell," Keith McCord greeted his son when he arrived for their curry night that evening. "Are you staying over tonight?"

"I was hoping to," McCord said. "I'll be quicker back at the station tomorrow, and I could murder a pint or two."

"Good. Have you charged the guy you caught yet? You had your doubts the last time we talked."

McCord shook his head.

"We had to release him. All the evidence is circumstantial; we can't establish a motive and he can't have abducted Amy."

"Abducted, your Amy? Oh, my God!"

"She isn't *my* Amy, Dad, and we've already found her. She had stumbled upon the murder scene and someone, probably the killer, kidnapped her and hid her on Andrew Campbell's estate. So, we're now looking at two guys who had a strong motive, and also at the older brother, John Campbell."

"The boyfriend of Amy's mother? The one from the McAdie case that you liked despite being a toff?"

"Yes, that one. He has motive, no alibi and knowledge of the estate."

"And you are not happy because Amy won't like it one bit if you suspect him," Keith observed shrewdly. "Difficult one."

"It was a mistake not even to consider him as a suspect. Maybe my DC is right; maybe I'm too involved in the case."

"Personally, I think you are too little involved." Keith winked. "Why don't you ask this Amy out at long last? It seems to me, admittedly from a distance, that you've been dancing around each other for months now."

"I don't think she's interested in me," McCord argued. He thought back to the hug that had never quite left his mind, and said, "She is just grateful that I found her."

"From what you're saying, she seems to be at the station an awful lot for someone who isn't interested," Keith observed.

"Why would she be? She's got the likes of Calderwood wrapped round her little finger."

"Not that I am an expert in women," Keith said, "but I think they prefer men who are stronger than those they can wrap around their little finger. You should tell her how you feel."

"And make things awkward between us? No way."

"Correct me if I'm wrong, but things seem to be awkward between you already. Has she not given you any sign of encouragement?"

McCord thought of her arms round his back, her body against his and her lips on his cheek.

"Maybe," he conceded.

"Then what are you waiting for, son?"

McCord dreaded these conversations that had become ever more frequent.

"Let's eat, Dad, before everything gets cold."

Chapter 20

DC Sutton obviously had put in a late shift because when McCord arrived at the station the following morning, he found a print-out of Kevin Jones' previous addresses on his desk.

"Come on, Calderwood," McCord said excitedly, "let's go."

Despite its name, 51B, Earl's Court, Liberton was a nondescript block of flats, painted in the depressing greyish-brown reserved for cheap housing. Kevin Jones's last known residence was on the second floor. The lights were on. In front of the ground-floor entrance, an empty double pram stuffed with shopping bags in the net underneath was waiting for the owner to come back to retrieve it. The door was wedged open, as if inviting them in. McCord and Calderwood exchanged a look and quietly hurried up the stairs. Once they were in front of Jones's door, there was no escape unless he jumped from the second floor. It occurred to McCord that neither of them carried a weapon nor wore a bulletproof vest, but since the murderer's preferred method of killing was hurling a rock, McCord fancied their chances. He pressed the bell and stood back. A distorted eyeball appeared at the spyhole.

"Who's there?" a suspicious voice called out.

"Police." McCord held up his warrant card.

They heard a key turning several times in the lock, then the door opened a few inches, revealing a security chain and a bespectacled young man eyeing them suspiciously.

"You don't look like police. Can I see your ID?"

McCord suppressed an oath. They were not sure what Kevin Jones looked like now, but he would have had to have put on at least six stones. McCord wondered if the man hovering behind the chain could have killed four men. It was possible, he supposed.

"We're looking for a Kevin Jones," he explained, holding his card up to the man's eyes so that he could examine it closely. "This is his last known address."

"He doesn't live here anymore. He left in July."

Calderwood grunted in frustration.

"Could we see your ID, please, sir?" McCord asked politely, not giving up just yet.

There was a shuffling sound in the corridor, and less than a minute later a chubby hand held out a passport to McCord.

"Steven Crawford," McCord read aloud for Calderwood's benefit. The passport had been issued eight years ago, and the picture on it showed a true likeness of the man.

"Sorry to bother you, sir," McCord said, handing the passport back. "Do you know where he went?"

"No, sorry," Steven Crawford said. "He hasn't kept in touch." He sounded hurt.

"So, you shared the flat a while?" McCord asked hopefully.

"For over three years, can you believe it? And not a sausage."

"Would you mind letting us in and telling us about him? Any little detail could help us with our investigation."

The chain rattled, the door opened, and Crawford invited them into the living room. It was warm with all three bars of the electric fire on. The host had obviously settled in front of the telly where a historic football match was showing. A small flicker of regret passed over his face as he switched it off.

"Would you like a tea or a coffee?"

The detectives accepted the coffee gratefully.

"What's he done?" Crawford shouted through the open door as he put the kettle on.

"His name came up in an investigation and he might be able to help us with our enquiries," McCord answered.

They heard cupboard doors opening and closing, and then Crawford came through with a tray. He handed them both a mug and, pointing to a plate heaped with biscuits and cake bites, sank into his armchair. McCord picked up a custard cream.

"How did you two meet?"

"We worked together at Burger King in the city centre, and when I got promoted to manager out here and needed someone to share the flat, he came along and got himself a job at the local inn."

"Did he say why he left?"

"Just that he had a new job somewhere else."

"Did you not ask him where?"

Crawford shrugged.

"He hated people being nosey. I knew that he would tell me what he wanted me to know, and that was that. He paid me the rent for an extra month because of the short notice. You hardly knew he was there, and he never caused any trouble."

"Did he leave any of his things?" Calderwood asked, clutching at straws.

"No, he didn't have much to begin with, only his art stuff and weights."

McCord thought of Robbie McArthur and his gym.

"Did he go to a gym called New You, by any chance?"

Crawford put down his mug.

"No, he did his training here. Quite obsessed he was, but it worked. He certainly put on some bulk. He tried to get me to join him, but I gave up after a while."

His sad smile told a whole story of failed attempts to get into shape.

"And his art? Was he an artist?"

"When he moved in, he told me he was interested in art, but he never seemed to paint anything, until later that is, roughly about the same time he started working out. After that, he was always on his easel but then he would tear the paintings up saying they were rubbish."

"And were they?" McCord asked.

"No idea, I know nothing about art. He loved German paintings for some reason, especially the expressionists I think they are called. I'd never heard of them before. He showed me a self-portrait of a guy called Otto something he had on the wall. Something like that would have given me nightmares. Red eyes and all about war and death. Not my taste at all but he said it was genius. Whatever. Odd in a way, because he was quite gentle. He would have loved a dog, but we're not allowed to have them here."

Calderwood shuffled impatiently in his seat, but McCord was fascinated.

"When you first met, did he say where he had come from?"

"He had stayed in the centre in a real shithole. I went there once. Incredible. They'll rent out a privy as a one-bedroom flat there and charge four hundred quid a month for it. He had a neighbour called Mrs Lockerbie who was nice, he said. I remember her name because a friend of my father's was killed by the plane that came down. Kevin never said much about himself, I just had the impression he had had a rough time in his past. Bit of a waste, really."

"What do you mean?" McCord asked.

"Well, working in a kitchen. He was very clever. He used to do *The Times* cryptic crossword in half an hour. I didn't even get it after he explained the clues to me."

McCord hesitated.

"Did you ever hear about the murder in a pub called The Shamrock in March?" McCord asked.

"Of course, it was all over the papers."

Crawford's eyes widened.

"You don't think that Kevin…? That's ridiculous."

"Why do you say that?" McCord demanded. "You said yourself that you hardly knew anything about him."

"True," Crawford admitted. "He was very private, but he seemed a genuinely nice guy. He was forever writing emails and letters for Amnesty International. He hated injustice. It doesn't make sense that he would kill somebody."

It did make sense if he hated the injustice done to himself enough, McCord thought, but did not say anything.

"Do you remember that day? Was he out that evening?" McCord asked.

Crawford shook his head.

"I don't remember. I often do shift work. And before you ask, I didn't see him put blood-stained clothes in the washing machine either."

"Did you notice a change in him around that time?" McCord persisted. "Anything?"

Crawford thought about this for a moment.

"I suppose around that time he started with his fitness regime; yes, because I remember he was lifting his weights and telling me he was up to 10kg when I asked him what he was doing for Easter, and he said he was staying here. He had always been quite dour, but suddenly he was all... fired up. I was wondering if he had his eyes on a girl because he was suddenly so concerned about his looks. That's also when he started painting again, but horrible stuff, all red and black splodges."

"Did he ever bring anybody here; a lover?"

Crawford shrugged.

"I don't think so, unless it was during my shifts." He shook his head, thinking back. "Nah, I can't see it."

He looked at McCord, who was waiting for him to elaborate. "He just didn't seem interested, in either women or men. Asexual, I suppose, you would call it."

"Thank you very much, Mr Crawford," McCord said, putting one of his cards on the coffee table. "You've been a great help. Should you think of anything else, please give me a call."

* * *

Outside, Calderwood looked at his boss. "And now? We're none the wiser; just a dead end."

"I know," McCord said. "But a picture is emerging. Round about the time of the first murder, Jones changed. Then there was a long spell when he did nothing, and now he is taking his tormentors out one by one. If that is the case, Andrew Campbell is in real danger."

"But where are we to look? We have no idea where he went," Calderwood said despondently.

"Sometimes one needs to go backwards to make progress." McCord checked the time on his watch. "Late morning is a good time to call on a respectable lady. Come on."

"Where are we going?" Calderwood asked, his face showing his confusion.

"That 'shithole' where Jones lived before he came here. Sutton traced him all the way back. And with a bit of luck, Mrs Lockerbie still lives there."

* * *

The bells of the Victorian flats at number 67, Lauriston Place were labelled A to F. To their delight, the name plate next to Flat B said 'Lockerbie'.

"Let's look at his place first. It's supposed to be 67 G," McCord said, checking his phone.

"Maybe Sutton got it wrong?" Calderwood suggested.

McCord just gave him a reproachful look. "Crawford called it a shithole, so it can't be one of these flats."

He stepped back from the building and noticed a rusty staircase leading to the basement. At the bottom was a small area, barely three square yards in size, surrounded by a wall, its only feature a battered metal door. It looked as if it had been a storage area in the past, but somebody had painted a wonky '67 G' on the outside. A little fir tree next to the door attempted to brighten up the dismal place.

There was no bell, so McCord knocked on the door, the bashed metal echoing through the tiny yard. Yet even three more attempts did not lead to success. Either there was nobody home, or they were not in the mood to receive visitors.

"Let's call on Mrs Lockerbie, then," McCord suggested.

Mrs Lockerbie in Flat B was pleased to receive a visitor and, after offering them a little sherry and home-made shortbread, she was only too happy to tell the detectives everything about the previous occupants of number 67 G.

"Shocking the way landlords exploit the housing shortage in this city. Sticking a human being into a dark, damp hole like that downstairs. It wouldn't surprise me if it was infested with rats. I sometimes go down and bring him some stew or cake, poor Mr Lidderdale. His wife threw him out, you know, but I suspect it was the drink that caused the end of the marriage. Women nowadays just don't put up with that kind of thing anymore, and rightly so. Still, it seems cruel–"

McCord could barely hide his impatience.

"We know that Kevin Jones moved here after leaving university," he interrupted her, "and from here, he went to live in Liberton. Is there anything you can tell me about him?"

Mrs Lockerbie looked offended by the detective's rudeness but was keen to give him her take on Kevin Jones.

"He was a poor, lost soul. When he first came, he hardly went out at all. Stuck all day in that room. One day I saw him come home, all skinny and sad, so I thought I'd bring him some dinner because men never look after themselves, do they, even the young ones, but he didn't answer the door. I was getting worried because he had just got in, so I knew he wasn't sleeping or anything. So, I called the landlord, and he came and unlocked the door. We found the lad on the floor, blood everywhere, I all but fainted with fright. He had cut his wrists, you see. We called an ambulance, and after a couple of days he was back and just carried on as before. I tried to talk to him, but he didn't say anything, he didn't even thank me for saving his life. And then, a few months later, he left. I was worried about him, but he never got in touch. Is he all right?"

"We don't know," McCord said, heaving himself out of the saggy sofa. "Thank you for your help. Good night."

* * *

"That poker game almost destroyed him," Calderwood remarked as they were walking towards their cars. "I wonder why he didn't go back to his parents. That's what I would have done."

"Well, let's ask them," McCord said, consulting his phone again. "Number 3, Eskdale Terrace, Bonnyrigg. Somehow, I don't believe he has gone home to Mummy and Daddy, but you never know."

Chapter 21

Eskdale Terrace was a neat and attractive street. The front lawns were mowed to a quarter inch of their death, and any weed daring to take root in the borders had been annihilated. Was it about control? McCord wondered. A proud but precarious existence, worked hard for and protected at all costs.

To McCord's relief, they found both Mr and Mrs Jones at home. Once they had inspected the detectives' IDs and been reassured that these were just routine enquiries, they were politely asked in and offered tea and coffee. It was the last thing McCord wanted but he needed background, an understanding of Kevin Jones, and he was not going to get it barging in and telling the parents that their son was suspected to be the serial killer everybody was talking about. Having taken a seat in the immaculate living room, it transpired that Mr Jones was a delivery driver on his day off, and Mrs Jones was not due to start her shift in a petrol station until 7pm.

Mr Jones put down his tea.

"I'm not sure how can we help you, Inspector."

"We would like to speak to your son, Kevin," McCord began. He saw how Mr Jones's face clouded over, and quickly finished his sentence. "His name came up in an investigation, and he might have vital information on the case we are working on. Is he here?"

Mrs Jones shook her head, eyes welling up.

"We haven't seen him for months," Mr Jones said, bitterly. "He's been travelling."

"Six months," Mrs Jones said accusingly in the direction of her husband. "He sends us a message every so often."

"Where has he gone?" McCord asked with a side glance at Calderwood. Had they got it all wrong?

"Somewhere in Australia, God knows where," Mr Jones said with a sweeping gesture of his hand that indicated that his son could just as well have gone to Mars.

"We understand that Kevin was at Edinburgh University; can you tell us anything about his time there?"

Mr Jones snorted.

"Don't get me started on that. Kevin had been hell-bent on going to university ever since he was sixteen. Art and Design, of all things. What do you want with that, I said to him, there are no jobs for students after they graduate, look at them all working at Burger King and McDonald's. No, I says, no way I'm putting my and your mum's hard-earned money into you painting pictures. If you're going at all, you're doing something that might earn you some money, like business management. He was not keen at first, so I tried to make him see that he'd be much better getting a decent job straight after school. But would he listen to me? Oh, no. One of his teachers, the one who had put the idea into his head, helped him with his applications for the business course, and he actually got into Edinburgh Uni."

There was some pride in his voice now, and McCord knew from experience the hopes and fears that sprout in the parents of a child who is the first in the family to go to university.

"He went off, got himself a job, but he could hardly make ends meet. His mum was pestering me day and night, so eventually I decided to help him out. Three thousand pounds, almost all our savings at the time."

He looked at McCord, expecting appreciation for the faith he had shown in his son's far-fetched dreams.

"Could he not have got a student loan?" McCord asked.

Mr Jones drew himself up with pride.

"We have never owed anybody anything," he declared. "What you can't pay for, you do without; that's always been my motto."

McCord moved onto the question he wanted answered most.

"Did Kevin make any friends at uni?"

"He talked about a few of them, how they were such men of the world, and how he wanted to be more like them."

McCord assumed that if the parents had known the names of these 'friends', they would have mentioned them by now as the papers had been full of them.

"And then one day, just before his first-year exams, he came by and told us, he had dropped out. Dropped out!" Mr Jones paused for effect. "I asked him where my money was, and he said he had lost it. Lost it! I wanted to know how, but he just carried on packing some bags, said he was sorry and left."

"Something bad had happened to him," Mrs Jones piped up, clearly angry at her husband. "He looked awful, but he wouldn't say what. He just said he needed to be on his own. He was away for a whole week; sick with worry I was."

She looked accusingly at McCord.

"I even went to the police, but they said there was nothing they could do, he was of age, and it was his right to leave home."

"Yes, rather than living here and save the money, he rented some place in the city and worked in the kitchen of some burger joint, just as I had predicted," her husband added.

"Ach, shut up!" his wife finally exploded. "What was he supposed to do? If you hadn't been so hard on him and so mean, he might have stayed rather than live in that terrible place! And now he has even left the country and gone to the other end of the world! Australia, he said. Such a huge place!"

Suddenly a glimmer of hope shone in her eyes.

"Inspector, if he is important to your inquiry, you will be looking for him, won't you? You'll find him?"

"We'll do our best," McCord said truthfully. "Would you mind if I had a look in his room? It might give us a clue as to where exactly he has gone."

"If his mother doesn't know where he is, I doubt you will have any more luck," said Mr Jones. "He was always a mummy's boy."

"Now that the detectives are here, they might as well have a look," Mrs Jones said, asserting herself. "Come on, I'll show you upstairs."

Kevin's room was still unchanged from the time he had been living at home: clean and tidy with matching curtains and bedcovers in blue geometrical pattern. A Manet print on the wall, a Leonardo da Vinci study of hands, and a drawing of his flying machine. Above the bed a large poster depicted a jetty leading out into a peaceful lake with hazy mountains in the distance.

"Lovely pictures," Kevin's mother commented, following McCord's gaze. "He was always passionate about art and full of dreams. Such a good boy, so gentle. But always at odds with his father."

"What did they argue about?"

"Money, mostly, I suppose. Kevin dreamed of a different life, and who could blame him. He wanted to go on courses, travel, be a painter, and we didn't have the money for that. You know what it's like, by the time you've paid the mortgage and the bills, there is nothing left."

McCord looked at a framed photograph showing Hamlet holding a skull.

"That was him in his last year at school. He is a very talented actor. There was even an article in the local newspaper mentioning him."

"Did he keep a diary?" McCord asked.

"No, he spent most of his evenings writing letters for Amnesty International. He has such a sense of justice, has our Kevin. He used to paint and draw all the time, but that terrible day when he had dropped out of uni, he took his sketchbooks, tore them all up and threw them in the bin."

McCord looked at Calderwood, but he shrugged as if to say that he could see nothing here that would help them further.

"I wonder if you have kept his baby teeth?" McCord asked.

Mrs Jones smiled.

"Of course, I have. He had the most beautiful teeth, and the tooth fairy came every time."

She disappeared into her bedroom and came back with a small enamel box containing half a dozen perfect little teeth.

"Could we please borrow one of them? I promise you will get it back very soon."

Mrs Jones pulled back her hand with the open box.

"Why would you want his tooth?" she cried in alarm. "You have found a body, haven't you, and now you want to check if it is him!"

"I swear," McCord said soothingly, "that there is no body we think might be Kevin's. A DNA profile might just help at some point. Remember, we both want to find him, don't we?"

Hesitantly, she picked out a tiny molar and handed it over to Calderwood, who carefully put it into a plastic evidence bag.

"If you could also lend me your phone, Mrs Jones," McCord asked. "I have a DC who is a wizard with technology, and she might be able to find out where Kevin sent his messages from. I'll get it back to you tomorrow at the latest."

Mrs Jones hesitated, but the temptation to know where her son was proved too great. Without a word, she pulled the mobile out of the pocket of her dressing gown and handed it to McCord.

"Thank you," McCord said. "I hope we find him soon."

* * *

Outside, walking back to their cars, McCord was quiet. Seduced by the prospect of easy money and people who lived a life he could only dream of, Kevin Jones had gambled away his only chance of a better future. McCord wondered what he would have done in Kevin's situation. Would he have told his dad? He doubted it but he was grateful that he had been brought up being loved so much that he would never have felt the need to impress people like Andrew Campbell and his entourage.

"What now?" Calderwood asked, looking crestfallen. "Somewhere in Australia!"

"Let's see what Sutton can do with the phone. If he is our killer, he is right here in Edinburgh."

Calderwood shook his head. "So far, his plan has worked out. All his tormentors dead, and he probably thinks their leader is still in a cell, accused of their murder. Unless he has found out that we released him, he has no reason to hang around now."

"I take your point," McCord said. "But Amy's kidnapping was not planned. He had to improvise." A terrible thought occurred to him. "She didn't see or hear anything, but does he know that? What if he still considers her a threat?"

"Then he would have killed her there and then," Calderwood argued, "but instead, he took considerable care not to hurt her unnecessarily. No, I think he's on the run."

McCord nodded. "Let's get back to the station. Send the still of the video to all ports and airports, and all railway stations as well."

Chapter 22

While McCord and Calderwood were in pursuit of Kevin Jones, Amy was back at the magazine. John had insisted she work on her article, and Amy felt she could not refuse although she would have preferred to stay at St Leonard's to be closer to the action.

She was pondering the new course the case had taken. She had until tomorrow to write her article, but what did she have? A dramatic kidnap where she was the victim, which was a good start. She could claim with a good conscience that Andrew Campbell had to be presumed innocent at this stage, but what should they reveal about the poker game video? Of course, it was pure gold to a journalist, but some innate decency made her hesitate to reveal to the public both the callousness of Andrew and the humiliation of the poor man filmed.

What if this episode had nothing to do with the case at all? It seemed likely to her that Andrew and his friends had made more enemies at university, and that Kevin was just one of them. In that case, he would be humiliated all over again; but if this poker game was the key to the murders, her revelations might jeopardise the investigation. There was nothing for it; they had to solve the case and find the killer first. And to do that, she needed caffeine.

"Fancy a coffee?" she called over to Martin.

"Yes, please," he said distractedly.

"What are you working on?" she asked, putting an americano on his desk.

He had been doodling on a pad that was filled with Scottish flags and little men in kilts.

"A cartoon on Scottish independence, or the lack thereof. I just can't get the people right."

To a stick man, he added broad shoulders and a six pack, and then a red mane and a bushy red beard and a kilt.

"What do you think?"

When Amy did not comment, he looked up. She stood there rigidly, staring at the picture.

"What's wrong?" Martin asked, now alarmed. "It's not that bad, is it?"

Amy shuddered as she came out of her trance.

"It's pure genius."

She kissed the bewildered cartoonist on his forehead and stormed out of the office, leaving the door swinging on its hinges as she ran out into the street towards St Leonard's.

* * *

"Really, Miss Thornton," McCord said with a mixture of ironic reproach and delight when Amy stormed into his office twenty minutes later, completely out of breath, "you can't expect us to find a person in less than one day when we only have a blurred, ten-year-old video and a name. But we are getting there, I promise!"

"I've got it," she panted, "I know. Duncan, can you put Kevin Jones's picture into an e-fit?"

"Sure," Calderwood shrugged, "just give me a minute."

While they were waiting, McCord observed the tiny droplets of sweat that had gathered on her forehead, her reddened cheeks and the sparkle in her eyes, and momentarily forgot all about the serial killer on the loose.

"Ready," Calderwood said. "What do you want me to add?"

Amy looked at the still. A boyish, clean-shaven face balancing on a thin neck.

"Make the neck thicker and add red hair and a red beard."

Calderwood clicked repeatedly on the picture.

The men stared at the screen.

"Bloody hell," was all McCord could say.

"Justin Torrence," Calderwood whispered.

"I suspect the first murder was completely opportunist," Amy said. "He happened upon Jordan Lamond, who had been at that dreadful poker game, and took his revenge. When he got away with it, he must have planned the other murders carefully; changing his appearance, getting the job on the estate, biding his time."

"And he didn't kill Andrew Campbell," McCord picked up the thread, "because for him he had something much worse in mind: the never-ending humiliation and degradation of life imprisonment. And his plan would have worked if–"

"If I hadn't been such a sentimental fool and gone back to the flat," Amy finished the sentence for him.

Calderwood was still shaking his head incredulously when McCord jumped up.

"Come on, we need to get to Carnethy and arrest Torrence! He would have heard this morning, or even last night, that Andrew is no longer a suspect and realised that his plan has failed. Maybe he's killed him already!"

They ran out to the Juke and had barely belted up when McCord pulled out into the main road.

"Calderwood, call for back up, and, Amy, call Andrew and his mother to warn them," McCord shouted over the noise of the engine that whined at being forced up to forty miles per hour in second gear.

Calderwood almost dropped his phone as McCord took a corner with screeching tyres.

"I really need one of those blue lights," he complained and honked the horn repeatedly to warn other drivers that he was about to jump a red light.

"I don't have their number," Amy shouted back. "I'll try John."

McCord said nothing, just grabbed the steering wheel tighter.

With the car swerving every few seconds, as McCord illegally overtook car after car on their way into Morningside, it took her three attempts to hit the correct button.

"I can't get through! I think he's meeting with a guy from an advertising agency today."

Amy clung on to the handle of the left rear door and prayed not to die in a car accident just yet. Especially since there was no point in hurrying. Kevin Jones aka Justin Torrence would not hang about for them to arrive. Seeing that his plan had failed, he would kill Andrew and disappear. How long does it take to bash somebody's head in, jump into a car and drive off? He knew the estate like the back of his hand, he would not need to come down the drive.

"Slow down!" she screamed when McCord drove full speed onto the A702 to a cacophony of horns. "It's too late anyway."

"We don't know that!" McCord shouted back.

The traffic through Morningside was nose to tail as always, and McCord had given up trying to overtake. Blissfully, the noise in the car subsided.

"Andrew Campbell is his special prize," McCord was thinking aloud. "He doesn't want him dead quickly; he wants him to suffer. He'll draw it out for as long as he can. He is very smart; he probably concocted a plan B as soon as you disrupted the first one. He only knows that we're no longer suspecting Andrew; he doesn't know that we're onto him."

Amy shuddered. She had thought that Andrew deserved whatever he got, but now that he was about to die, she hoped desperately that they would get there in time. The traffic thinned as they left the centre heading out towards the Pentlands. Amy quickly typed a message to John telling him to warn Andrew and his mother that Justin Torrence was the killer.

"Step on it," Amy said and clung on to the door even tighter.

Chapter 23

The delicately pink gravel sprayed in all directions as McCord skidded to a halt in front of the stone steps. Andrew's cabriolet was neatly parked to the side, but the Land Rover was nowhere to be seen.

Calderwood was first out of the Juke and at the front door.

"Police!" he shouted, hammering at the front door. "Open up!"

There was no answer. Calderwood took another breath, but no sound came out as McCord squeezed past him and turned the huge brass wreath that was screwed to the varnished wood. The door swung open into the dark hall.

"Mr Campbell? Mrs Campbell?" McCord's voice seemed to disappear in the huge space and the rooms adjoining it.

"Shall I take this end with Amy, and you check the east wing?" Calderwood suggested.

"Nobody is going anywhere on their own," McCord decided. "We're sticking together."

They checked the drawing room. There was no sign of a fight, every cushion was in its place. Back in the hall, McCord pointed to the right, and they ran down a long corridor, listening for any sounds. McCord tried not to double over with a stitch in his side, and Amy was about to ask Calderwood to slow down when they heard a squeak and a clicking sound. They all stopped. McCord put a finger to his lips and motioned the others to let him go first. Ahead of them the corridor ended, and another started at right angles. With Calderwood and Amy behind him, McCord peeked round the corner to find the barrel of a rifle pointing at his head. He pulled back instinctively when a strident voice called out.

"DI McCord! For God's sake, what took you so long?!"

Amy leant against the wall, panting, and McCord allowed himself to bend over and press his hand on the searing pain in his side, so Calderwood was the only one fit to face the enemy.

"Mrs Campbell," he said, only slightly out of breath, "is everything okay?"

"Okay?" Edith Campbell mimicked him sarcastically. "A lunatic is trying to kill my son, and you're asking me if everything is *okay*?"

Around the corner, McCord and Amy shared a smile. He pulled himself up and joined his DC.

Edith Campbell had risen from the chair she had placed in front of Andrew's bedroom door and lowered the rifle she was holding.

"I would have thought the message a joke if it hadn't come from John. Justin Torrence a serial killer? And now he is after Andrew?"

"I'm afraid it's true. Are you in there, Mr Campbell?"

"Yes," came the reluctant answer from inside the room.

They heard the scraping of heavy furniture across the floor, then a key turned in the lock and the door opened. Andrew Campbell, also clutching a shotgun, appeared on the threshold.

Relief, fear and embarrassment oscillated in his face.

"What is going on? Is this an elaborate joke?" he asked.

"I'm afraid not," McCord said. "Where is Torrence?"

"I have no idea, I've been stuck in this room, remember?"

The old arrogance was already reasserting itself.

"Guarded by the lady of the house," McCord could not stop himself from pointing out.

"This is all nonsense, anyway," Mrs Campbell declared. "I simply can't imagine that Justin would ever harm us."

"Well, let's be grateful that he hasn't done so yet, shall we?"

The wailing of sirens and the chopping of a helicopter sounded through the sash windows.

"Here's the back up," McCord observed. "Hopefully, in time to catch him. DC Calderwood, accompany Mrs Campbell to the drawing room. Mr Campbell, I think you might want to change your trousers before joining them. I'll be waiting outside."

Andrew Campbell slammed the door in McCord's grinning face.

* * *

After McCord had instructed the troops to search the estate for any sign of Kevin Jones, aka Justin Torrence, and had organised roadblocks looking out for the estate's Land Rover, he and Andrew joined the others in the drawing room.

"I still don't understand," Edith Campbell complained. "Why is all this happening?"

McCord turned to Andrew Campbell.

"Would you like to explain, Mr Campbell?"

"Not really," Andrew Campbell replied. "Are you still going on about that silly poker game?"

"Yes, that silly poker game," McCord said coldly.

"What *are* you talking about?" Edith Campbell said. "I demand to know what you are talking about!"

"Very well, if you insist. DC Calderwood, show them."

Calderwood tapped on his phone and held it out to Edith Campbell.

Andrew looked decidedly uncomfortable now.

"Is this really necessary, Inspector?" he asked.

"Oh, I think so," McCord replied.

Calderwood played the video. When it had ended, nobody spoke.

Eventually, McCord broke the silence.

"Because of this 'silly poker game', as you call it, a man lost what for him was a fortune, his academic future and, what was probably worst, his dignity. As a result, he attempted suicide but was rescued by a caring neighbour. Estranged from his parents, whom he was unable to face, he spent years hiding from the world. He had been utterly humiliated. He scraped a living working in the kitchen of a burger joint.

"And then one day, he bumps into Jordan Lamond in the toilet of a pub. We don't exactly know what happened there. I wouldn't be surprised if Lamond said something he thought was funny, and Jones snapped. He bashed Lamond's head into the sink and got away with it. That must have given him the idea to take revenge on the whole lot of you.

"But he is smart; he realised he would not get away with it so easily again. He hatched a devilish and ingenious plan. He disappeared and turned himself into Justin Torrence, working out, growing his hair and a beard and staking out his future victims. He manipulated you, Mrs Campbell, into giving him a job on the estate where, like a spider in its web, he could observe everything. I bet there was never anything wrong with your car, and he guessed correctly that you would never say no to a bit of cheap labour.

"You, Mr Campbell, never recognised him because then and now, the Kevin Joneses of this world are too irrelevant to be noticed unless they are used for a bit of sport. And when he was ready, he picked off your friends one by one, waiting behind a shrub for Robbie McArthur, posing as a pizza delivery man with an invented order for Zac Walker and a potential buyer for

Alex Buchan. But you, Mr Campbell, were the prize. The leader of the pack, the alpha male, the one with the amusing idea to put a working-class kid in his place. A quick bash over the head would not do for you. You had to suffer the way he did, in squalor and never-ending humiliation. Had it not been for Miss Thornton stumbling into the murder scene, his plan would have worked, and you would have gone down for murder. It was a nice touch how he gave you an alibi while he was killing the others, only for it to crumble under my interrogation and leave you as our prime suspect at the end.

"But Miss Thornton's observations at the shop told us that you could not have abducted her and were unlikely to be the killer. Ironically, if he had killed her, he would have got away with it because we would not have known that she had gone to the shop and seen the body of Alex Buchan before you arrived. I've been wondering why he didn't kill her, and even made an effort to keep her comfortable. I think he sees himself as an avenging angel who dispenses justice and only kills those who he thinks deserve it. If he was still around earlier, he didn't kill you because you were surrounded by innocent people he didn't want to harm."

His phone rang. He listened, thanked the caller and hung up.

"They've found lots of red hair in the sink in the estate office. All the cash has gone. The Land Rover has been abandoned on the edge of the estate, near a bus stop. It looks like he's done a runner."

McCord looked at the stunned face of Edith Campbell.

"And he left a note saying, 'Prepare for death'. So, now we have an extremely clever serial killer who is plotting another way to get to the last of his tormentors and so complete his revenge. And we have no idea what his plan is. If I were you, Mr Campbell," McCord said to

Andrew, "I'd be extremely careful until we have arrested Jones."

Edith Campbell's steely countenance had finally broken. Her voice was brittle as she turned to her younger son.

"I thought I was going to die of shame when you were arrested and the papers were accusing you of murder, but at least I knew you were innocent. All that was nothing compared to the shame I feel now. *This*" – she pointed with disgust at Calderwood's phone which still showed the last still of the video – "is a disgrace. *You* are a disgrace. Get out of my sight."

Andrew Campbell looked as if he had been slapped and he saw no sympathy in the eyes he met. He rose stiffly, his head held high, and stalked out of the room.

McCord cleared his throat and motioned to Calderwood that it was time to leave.

"Well, I suppose we'd better go and find Jones. For Mr Campbell's protection I'll leave an officer here. Would you have a spare room for him, Mrs Campbell?"

"Of course," she said quietly. "Thank you, Inspector."

Chapter 24

Amy had gone back to the magazine and spent the rest of the day feverishly typing her weekend feature about the 'Rock Killer' as he was known by now. The city was abuzz with excitement as everybody was looking for a muscular man of medium height with grey eyes, whose hair could be any length and colour by now. She recounted the whole story, but did not mention the video for John's sake, who, after watching it, had retired to his office without a word and not reappeared since. Martin fluttered around Amy's desk making irritating noises until she relented and finally told him what had happened.

"How awful," he whispered. "To think about the tragedy this egotistical, heartless man has caused. All those lives destroyed, and even John under suspicion!"

"What do you mean?" Amy asked. "How was John under suspicion?"

Martin's face became even more pinched than usual.

"Nothing, I mean, I'm sure everyone was under suspicion at some point, weren't they?"

"Nonsense," Amy cut him short. "What do you mean?"

"It's nothing, really, just when I went to the station to impress upon DI McCord the importance of starting the search for you immediately, he asked me about John, if he had changed at all, if he had been weird; and John told me McCord had asked Valerie if he had been in town the evening you disappeared."

Amy's eyes narrowed.

"Did he indeed. How interesting. I think I'm going to have a word with DI McCord right now."

"I'm sure there is no need," Martin said, afraid that he might have squashed the tiny spark that had appeared between Amy and the detective. "I probably misinterpreted what he said. And Valerie, too," he added, in a panic-stricken voice. "And anyway, you need to finish your article by tonight!"

But Amy was already out of the door.

* * *

McCord was drumming another nervous gallop on his desk, waiting for news from the search team. A phone call with Andrew Campbell had confirmed that

Jones had used the estate account in Andrew's absence to withdraw £5,000 in cash.

The red hair Justin Torrence had shaved off had been sent for DNA testing to be compared with Kevin Jones's molar. McCord had no doubts as to the outcome. A pair of shoes that was found in Torrence's room was the same size as the footprint next to Zac Walker's body, but the boots were not there, and McCord was sure the ones used in the murder had been destroyed by now.

Calderwood had organised a surveillance car to go to Eskdale Terrace in case Jones got in touch with his parents. The bus driver on the route past the estate had been found and interviewed but remembered nothing about the passenger who had got on at the bus stop because he had just been told about a new set of roadworks that was going to make him late.

"Damn," McCord said. "I fear he has slipped through the net. Who knows where he is holed up by now. He has cash and all the time in the world to wait until the fuss has died down, and then to target Andrew Campbell. We can't keep an officer there forever either. And the longer it goes on, the more time he has to think, to plan and to prepare. I don't like it one bit."

Calderwood nodded his agreement.

"At least there is hope that he will not hurt anybody apart from Andrew Campbell."

"Yes," McCord said. "But as much as I despise Andrew Campbell, I definitely don't want his body on a slab in Edinburgh. Maybe we should suggest to Mrs Campbell that she sends him abroad?"

"But the only way to catch Jones is through Campbell, and we don't want four unsolved murders on our stats either," Calderwood said.

"You're beginning to sound like the Super," McCord growled. "You'll go far."

"In my humble opinion, you went far too far as it is." Amy's furious voice sounded from the door. "What were you thinking, McCord, suspecting *John*?! After all we've been through together – how *could* you?!"

Calderwood was squirming in his chair. Denial seemed futile, and he had just opened his mouth to confess when McCord spoke up.

"Because I couldn't *not* consider him, even if it was for the shortest time. Everything pointed to the Campbell connection, and we had agreed that it was not Andrew. A policeman has to follow the evidence, not his heart."

"Clearly." Amy's voice dripped with sarcasm. "What you're saying is that if I hadn't found that video, you would have thrown John in a cell?"

"Believe me, I took no pleasure in any of this," McCord said. "But with you having disappeared without a trace, no scenario was off limits."

He caught himself in time not to mention that he'd had John under surveillance. One could be too honest.

Amy harrumphed in a most unladylike manner and dithered over whether to make a retreat and continue with her article or hang around a bit longer. The decision was easy.

"Any sightings of Jones?"

"Nothing yet," Calderwood said quickly, looking relieved that Amy's wrath had passed him by thanks to McCord having taken the hit. "We've produced several pictures using different hairstyles and distributed them round the city. Pity we don't know of any distinguishing marks."

"He should have a scar on each wrist," McCord thought aloud, "from when he tried to kill himself."

Calderwood made a call at once to add this to the description of the wanted man.

There was an awkward moment as both McCord and Amy were at a loss of what to say.

"Calderwood and I were just discussing how to catch Jones," McCord said, breaking the silence. "The surest way is when he comes near Andrew Campbell."

"You mean using him as bait?" Amy asked.

"We can't do that," Calderwood said, shocked.

"It wouldn't be the first time we caught a killer by doing that," Amy remarked, looking at McCord. "And it worked."

"Don't even think about it," McCord said firmly. "That crazy scheme of mine almost got you killed."

Amy closed her eyes. "I remember."

Her scar itched every time a sound or sight took her back to that moment.

"Not that Andrew doesn't deserve a bit of worrying after everything he did, but he can't live in a state of anxiety indefinitely," McCord said. "And as Calderwood put it, it does not look good on our stats. The Super's been at me again. He's not at all happy, which means I'm not happy either. We'll just *have* to find Jones."

Chapter 25

"I'm concerned about Andrew," John said, confiding in Amy over a coffee the next morning. "I keep thinking Justin, or rather Kevin Jones, will get to him somehow."

After feverishly typing her article long into the small hours for the weekend edition, she had indulged in a lie-in before coming back into the office.

"The protection officer is there all the time. While he's there, Andrew will be safe," Amy reassured him.

"But how long can they keep this going? What if the police don't find Jones? Mama says Andrew pretends not to care but is in a constant panic."

"Try not to worry too much," she told him and planted a kiss on his furrowed forehead.

She checked the time and jumped up.

"I'd better go to the station and see if there is any news. They'll be doing a brainstorming session on how to catch Jones."

"Do you not think you should just let the police get on with their job?" John replied. "Remember you have a job to do here as well."

"But McCord needs my help."

"Will you be back after lunch?" John called after her, but she had already banged the door shut after her.

* * *

When Amy knocked on the open door of McCord's office, he was on the phone. He put a finger to his lips, so she tiptoed in and gave Calderwood a silent wave.

"Right, you do that. I'll be there as soon as I can."

He lowered his phone. Amy had seen the look before; the hunter closing in on the prey.

"We have a possible sighting. Burger King on Princes Street. The manager was interviewing for a vacancy and noticed a scar on his right wrist and the grey eyes. He thinks it could be Jones although he had dark hair and a moustache. Let's go."

The detectives rushed downstairs into the car park, Amy hot on their heels.

"He'll have long gone by the time we get there, even with the way you drive," Amy complained.

McCord ignored the last comment.

"Some officers are already on their way, and we're trying to seal off the area around it. The manager is switched on. He told Jones, if it *was* him, that he was in the running for the job and should wait in the restaurant until he had finished the other interviews. He said he would tell him in half an hour or so, and then he phoned us. Let's hope that it is Jones and that he doesn't get suspicious."

"Why would he stay in the city centre, right under our noses?" Calderwood wondered.

"He probably has no transport," McCord said whilst driving up Nicholson Street. "In the centre, among thousands of people, he is less likely to draw attention to himself than in a quieter area. And he's more likely to get away if he is spotted."

His phone was mounted on its stand in front of the dashboard, so his team could keep him updated.

"Two constables from the local police are about to enter the restaurant," a female voice said.

"Are they in plain clothes?" McCord asked.

"Not sure."

"Well, check!" McCord raised his voice impatiently. "If he sees them in uniform, he'll smell a rat and run. Quick!"

The phone went silent.

McCord was crossing South Bridge, and Amy could not help looking out for her mum's old shop where Jones had abducted her. But before they had reached it, the voice came back.

"They were in uniform. We've just caught them before going in. They're now walking down the street."

McCord exhaled.

They had passed the shop and were crossing North Bridge when the phone lit up again.

"Waiter says suspect paid for his meal and left restaurant through the back door."

"I hope you had somebody posted there?" McCord demanded.

There was a moment's silence.

"Sorry, sir, not yet."

"Well, hurry up and search the area!" McCord shouted. "Mind, he might have taken off the black moustache. And alert the staff at Waverley!"

They were about to turn into Waterloo Place. McCord was swearing at traffic lights, one-way systems, cars and, most of all, people. Suddenly, he pulled the Juke up the pavement and jumped out.

"Get out," he shouted at his passengers. "He'll be trying to get into the station and onto a train. Maybe we can catch him before he reaches the stairs!"

They turned left and jogged along Princes Street, scanning the crowds sauntering towards them but all they could see were ordinary people going about their business, and, of course, tourists.

McCord's phone pinged.

"Lost him, sir. Checking the station now."

"Damn." McCord slowed down to catch his breath. "I bet he's on a train and gone. He always seems one step ahead of us."

* * *

The officers interviewing staff at Waverley had no encouraging news either. Nobody had jumped the barriers or behaved in a conspicuous manner. They had just begun checking CCTV footage, but McCord secretly thought it was a waste of time. Jones was gone and would reappear in a different guise.

"He must have bought a ticket in advance, just in case," McCord said to Calderwood.

His phone pinged.

"It's from Sutton. She's got something. I need to get back to the station."

* * *

Twenty minutes later McCord was at DC Sutton's workstation.

After knocking on the outer defensive wall, he moved carefully towards her desk.

DC Sutton did not turn away from her screen, but a slight tensing of her body told McCord that she knew he was there. She pointed to Mrs Jones's phone that lay in front of her.

"Message sent from the centre of Edinburgh. Another one has just come in."

McCord could barely refrain himself from grabbing the phone.

"What does it say?"

"'Hi Mum, tell Dad I put the money I owe him back into his account. Things are going well. Look after yourselves, Kevin.'"

"Great, thanks, DC Sutton. Was that sent from the same location?"

Sutton tilted her head.

"Don't know. Different dumb phone. Need to trace first."

McCord's hopes dissipated. By the time they had found out, Jones would have a different phone.

"Could you trace it for me anyway? And then" – he lowered his voice – "could you check the bank account of Mr Jones senior and see if the money is there and where it came from? I don't have a warrant yet, so no need for anybody else to know."

* * *

Back at the office, McCord's mobile rang. Why was there never a moment when he had time to think?

"DI McCord," he said irritably.

"It's Edith Campbell here," the caller said.

McCord's surprise was tinged with guilt. The Super had told him to phone to apologise for treating Andrew like a suspect, but he could not help feeling that none of this would have happened if Andrew Campbell hadn't been such a bully, and that he had come off lightly in the end.

"I hope you don't mind me calling you on your mobile; John gave me your number. I wondered if there was any news?" Edith Campbell asked.

Her voice had lost its coldness; he had saved her from the onslaught of the press and now was the only person who could protect her wayward but beloved son.

"We've had a possible sighting, but nothing has come of it yet," McCord said cautiously.

"I do hope you catch that man soon. This has been an absolute nightmare. At least the magazine is not going to publish the video, which I'm very relieved about, I must admit. It was very decent of Miss Thornton not to insist on it."

"Yes, she is a remarkable woman," McCord agreed.

"I know the case is not over for you, and that madman is still out there, but we wanted at least to celebrate Andrew's release from prison. We are having dinner tonight at eight; John, Miss Thornton and her mother, and you, to thank you all for your support and keeping Andrew safe. Would you be able to come?"

McCord had very mixed feelings about a dinner with the Campbells, but the thought of Amy being there and the Super's certain approval made the decision easy.

"I would be delighted," he said, thinking what Calderwood would say. "Eight o'clock. Thank you very much, Mrs Campbell."

Calderwood looked at McCord across his desk. "You're moving into the upper echelons of society, I see. Dinner invitation from Mrs Campbell, is it?"

McCord nodded.

"Blimey! Who else is going to be there?" Calderwood asked.

"Just the family," McCord said, vaguely. "I'm sure that it was John's idea."

Or Amy's, he thought.

"Anyway, we need to get to Eskdale Terrace quickly. I don't want Jones to become suspicious because his mother doesn't answer his message."

* * *

The surveillance car was parked roughly ten yards down from the Joneses' front door. Ignoring the driver in case Kevin Jones was watching the house, McCord rang the bell. Mrs Jones had just come back from the shops. To McCord's relief, Mr Jones was at work.

He did not wait until Mrs Jones had made them coffee and tea but handed her the phone as soon as they had entered the hall.

"Here is your phone back, Mrs Jones."

She grabbed it eagerly and looked at her messages.

"There," she beamed. "He has sent a message today. He says he has paid back the £3,000 his dad had given him. See? He must be doing well down under."

She quickly typed a reply and sent it with a smile.

McCord felt a familiar tightness in his stomach.

"Mrs Jones, we have traced the last messages back to Edinburgh. Kevin is here in the city and has been here ever since he left university."

Mrs Jones slowly looked up from her phone.

"In Edinburgh?" she whispered. "He can't be. He would have come to see me."

McCord swallowed.

"Why don't we go into the lounge?"

Once seated, he turned to her.

"I'm sorry to have to tell you, but there is mounting evidence that Kevin is the man we are looking for in connection with the recent spate of murders. We believe that he is here in Edinburgh, planning to commit another murder, and we must find him before he does."

Mrs Jones kept shaking her head.

"No," she whispered, "no. You are making a terrible mistake."

"You were right when you said that something awful happened to Kevin when he was at university. He lost three thousand pounds at poker and was deeply humiliated by a group of men he thought were his friends. He could not face the world after that and tried to commit suicide."

Mrs Jones covered her mouth with her hands. The sounds she made reminded McCord of a bird he had once seen gripped in the jaws of a cat. He still felt sick at the memory of wringing the fragile neck to end its agony.

"Kevin was saved by a neighbour and stayed in a rented room in the city. After that, he lived in Liberton for a while. In March, he met one of the men in a pub, and something must have snapped. He killed him. He then decided to take revenge on all the men who ruined his life. Of these men, only one is still alive, and Kevin has threatened to kill him as well."

Mrs Jones was sobbing now, shaking her head incessantly.

"The best way to help your son now is to work with us, so that we can prevent another tragedy," McCord said gently. "Is there anything you can tell me that might help us find him?"

Mrs Jones dried her tears and stood up straight, suddenly all meekness gone.

"No," she declared.

McCord sighed.

"I fear that the press will start to bother you soon. It's best if you say nothing. If they trespass onto your property or frighten you, give me a call."

He offered his card, but she folded her arms defiantly. He placed it on the table instead.

"Maybe you could stay with relatives or friends for a while?" he suggested.

She looked at him, and the despair in her eyes made him wish he had it all wrong.

"I am so very sorry," he said again as he left the house.

* * *

On his way to the car, he received a message from Sutton. This confirmed what he knew already.

> *Traced William Gibbs' car. Not at Dunsapie Loch at time of murder.*

McCord sighed. He would have to phone Gibbs to tell him that he was no longer under suspicion.

Chapter 26

With Lucy's help, Carnethy House had regained some of its former glory. The dining room was illuminated by not one but two chandeliers as well as an eighteenth-century candelabrum at the centre of the table, set with delicate china and crystal glasses. McCord was greeted with a handshake by Mrs Campbell and the men, and with a fleeting kiss on the cheek first by Valerie and then a lingering one by Amy, which left him slightly dizzy.

After they had all been given a glass of champagne, apart from McCord, who, since he was driving, had to make do with orange juice, Mrs Campbell tapped on her glass.

"Let's drink to everybody who has helped clear Andrew's name."

They all drank to that and then sat down to an excellent dinner. Mrs Campbell asked Valerie about her new business venture and was mightily impressed when she heard about her plans for a fashion show in Edinburgh. She looked with renewed respect at her older son who recently had been a blessing rather than a constant source of worry.

With every course and the accompanying wines, Andrew lost some of his new-found humility. He entertained them with stories from prison and boasted he had never been truly worried because he believed in the Scottish justice system.

"And now I even have my very own bodyguard," he said with a laugh.

"I don't see the funny side of this," his mother said sharply. "If it weren't for your despicable behaviour, none of this would have happened."

"Now don't blow things out of proportion, Mama. The guy lost at a poker game; if you play for money, you've got to take it on the chin. And if he had gone to a private boys' school, he would have been used to having his pants pulled down. It's not my fault if the moron went mental. But thanks to DI McCord and Amy, he's done a runner."

He lifted his glass with an ironic bow to them both.

McCord exchanged a look with Amy that confirmed that she shared his thoughts; John and Valerie stared determinedly at their empty plates.

"Well, if I were him," Edith Campbell declared, "I would not have slunk away so cowardly. I would have made sure you got your comeuppance, my boy. I thought that a night in prison would have taught you a lesson, but obviously not."

"Now, now, Mama," Andrew said, offended. "It sounds as if you are on the side of a deranged serial killer rather than your son's. I think it's time for an after-dinner drink."

* * *

While Lucy was clearing the table, they moved into the drawing room. Outside the wind was howling and throwing torn-off leaves and twigs against the windows. All the diners apart from McCord had consumed copious amounts of alcohol and were much more relaxed around each other. John lifted the mood by telling the party how one of Phoebe Smythe-Tennyson's bulls had escaped his enclosure, raided her front garden and given her the fright of her life by looking straight at her through the window.

McCord, still clutching his non-alcoholic beer from dinner, was the only one who did not laugh. He caught Amy's eye who looked at him quizzingly. He shrugged. Something Edith Campbell had said was bouncing backwards and forwards in his brain as if desperate to tell him something. Kevin Jones had meticulously planned and coolly executed four murders; surely, he would have considered different options in case something went wrong. The way he had disappeared so easily in a relatively small city, well equipped with cash and different disguises, was not just down to luck, it was down to preparation. And he would never let off the worst of his tormentors so lightly. He put himself in Jones's position. What would he have done?

Only half-consciously he heard the drinks being dished out; port for everybody, while Andrew poured himself a generous measure of his favourite, the twenty-year-old Laphroaig, which, as he proudly declared, was far too fiery for anybody else in this household to drink.

"Well, cheers," Andrew said.

With one leap, McCord was off the sofa and knocked the glass out of Andrew's hand as he was just about to take a sip.

"What the–" Andrew gasped.

"Don't drink any of that," McCord shouted. "It's poisoned."

"What?" everyone said in unison, staring at McCord as if he had gone mad.

He looked slightly embarrassed now; such theatrical performances were not normally his style.

"Sorry," he mumbled. "Mrs Campbell, did you tell Jones that Andrew was about to be released before you went to pick him up?"

Edith Campbell thought for a moment.

"Yes, I saw him straight after Alan, our lawyer, phoned. He was just outside, and I was so excited that I told everybody."

McCord just nodded and went out into the hall to make a phone call.

* * *

The others were left sitting in the drawing room, at a loss for words. Everybody had put their drink down, eyeing them suspiciously.

Amy's mind was racing. What was it that had occurred to McCord?

"Of course!" Amy exclaimed again. "How fiendishly clever! But not too clever for DI McCord," she added proudly.

"What is?" Valerie demanded. "Stop talking in riddles, girl!"

"It had always been Jones's plan to make Andrew suffer the most because he was the leader of that group of friends he tried to belong to. But when I was found, he must have realised that sooner or later McCord would figure out that Andrew could not be the killer and that he would be released, which is exactly what happened. So, Jones had to think of another plan.

"He had to make a quick escape, but he was not going to give up on his revenge. He probably knew that

Andrew was fond of this whisky and the only person in the household to drink that particular one, so he laced the Laphroaig in the decanter with poison – I guess some pesticide from the estate."

She looked up expectantly as McCord re-entered the room, putting his phone away.

"I've got a friend in the toxicology lab. He'll test the samples first thing tomorrow morning. Mrs Campbell, could you find us some small, clean jars or containers we could use?"

Edith Campbell quickly rose to find Lucy.

"Don't you think you are overreacting, McCord?" Andrew objected.

"Maybe I am," the detective conceded, "but do you really want to take that risk?"

Andrew sighed in frustration.

"Right, can you think of anything else that only you eat, drink or use? That would be a good place to start."

Andrew laughed.

"I really don't know…"

"Toothpaste, toiletries, medication?" McCord suggested, struggling to remain patient. "Basically, everything in your bathroom cabinet. And your car. Do not use it until it has been checked over. Jones knows about cars, remember? That's how he got this job, by engineering a breakdown and then fixing it. My friend says it would help if he had some idea what he is looking for. Is there anywhere on the estate where you keep poisonous substances? Pesticides, fertilisers?" he asked.

Andrew had suddenly sobered up. "Come with me, I'll show you."

Chapter 27

The next morning, McCord was flicking through the files of the four murders, as if some hidden clue he had missed might jump out at them.

"Has it occurred to you two that we have not one single morsel of physical evidence against Jones?" he asked Calderwood and Amy.

Amy had been unable to concentrate on her article on a spate of burglaries in Morningside and had persuaded John that she would be much better helping McCord to find the man trying to kill his brother.

"Surely, the DNA of Jones's tooth will match the red hair left by Torrence?" Calderwood pointed out.

"That will prove that Jones and Torrence are one and the same person, but not that he is the killer."

"Has Sutton found anything on the call made to Buchan that lured him to the shop?"

"It was the same number the estate agent gave me; the mystery client who only gave a false name and number, and only wanted to deal with Buchan. I have no doubt it was Jones, but the phone is no longer traceable. Sutton says he keeps buying cheap pay-as-you-go dumb phones and chucks them after use. Did we find out anything about the fake pizza delivery?"

Calderwood rummaged through the papers on his desk.

"Yes, sort of. A couple of colleagues went round all the pizza places in the area. A delivery motorbike was stolen from a pizza place near Walker's flat but later returned undamaged, so they did not report it at the time. The manager knew which bike it was, but it has been used many times and cleaned since. It has been taken into forensics anyway."

McCord nodded approvingly. "Good. I doubt very much that Jones left any traces, but one never knows."

Distracted by an alert, he opened his emails, read the latest one and sat back.

"Bloody hell."

Amy and Calderwood both jumped up and took up position left and right of McCord, bending over his shoulders to see the screen.

"You need to phone Andrew – now!" Amy exclaimed.

"I am going to. I'm just trying to think what he should do next. Any bright ideas?"

After a moment's silence, Amy shook her head. The tip of her swinging ponytail brushed McCord's neck, making it difficult for him to concentrate on Andrew Campbell's rescue.

"Calderwood?"

"No idea. I'm glad I'm not in his position, anyway."

McCord sighed.

"You're both pretty useless this morning," he said and clicked on Andrew Campbell's number. "I hope he has done what he was told."

Andrew Campbell answered immediately. He sounded breathless.

"Any news?"

"I'm afraid so," McCord said, trying to sound calm. "I've just got the preliminary findings. The official report comes later, but–"

"What does it say?"

"There was strychnine in the whisky and arsenic in your toothpaste. The arsenic would not have killed you straightaway, but over a longer period of time. There was also sulphuric acid in your shampoo, which would have been very unpleasant if you had washed your hair with it."

It was quiet at the other end, and when Andrew Campbell spoke again, his voice was shaky.

"And the strychnine in the whisky?"

"Would have killed you after fifteen minutes or so. Painful spasms, inability to breathe" – he read on silently – "never mind the details."

McCord had thought he would enjoy being right and putting the fear of death into Andrew Campbell, but instead his stomach felt like a lead ball.

"What am I to do now?" Andrew croaked.

"I don't know," McCord said honestly. "I suppose, the first thing is to clear out your shed. These substances should not be standing around on a shelf in jam jars. Have our forensic people arrived to check the car?"

"Yes, they've been here a while. Hang on, one of them wants to speak to you."

The cheery voice of the forensics team leader boomed through the room. "DI McCord? Looks like you were right. The brakes have been tampered with. No prints so far."

"Thanks. Keep looking. A red hair would be great."

The man at the other end laughed.

"We should be so lucky. This guy is good. I'll hand you back to Mr Campbell."

There was a shuffling sound, then Andrew Campbell was back on the line.

"I take it, you heard," McCord said. "For now, you have to assume that Jones has left more unpleasant surprises. Remember, he had ample time to lay traps. Don't go anywhere, and I mean *anywhere*, without your protection officer, be careful about what you eat and drink and stay away from people you don't know. Jones was an amateur actor and is clearly very good at disguising himself."

"Right," Andrew said, "I will." He ended the call.

"He could have at least thanked you for saving his life," Amy said pointedly. "Do you think Mrs Campbell is in danger?"

McCord shook his head.

"I still believe that Jones has his own warped moral code, which only allows him to harm Andrew; on the other hand, his plan has failed, the police are looking everywhere for him. He might get desperate and try anything. I'm afraid we all need to try to think like him. What other traps could he have set before he left?"

"Maybe Andrew should move out until we've found Jones," Calderwood said.

"I suppose a smaller flat would be easier to monitor," McCord agreed. "Amy, why don't you suggest that to John and his mother?"

McCord's phone pinged; he had just received another message.

"What now?" Calderwood asked.

"The Super wants to see me," McCord sighed, rising from his chair. "If anything comes up, feel free to text me at once."

* * *

Superintendent Gilchrist was in a belligerent mood.

"DI McCord, any progress with finding this madman?"

"All airports, ferries and railway stations have been alerted and leaflets distributed all over the town. We've also set up a Twitter account and Facebook page to pass on any new information to the public quickly. We almost caught him yesterday when he–"

"Almost," Gilchrist barked. "Almost is no use, is it, DI McCord. Is there any evidence yet to satisfy the procurator fiscal?"

"We are comparing DNA from Jones with the hair left by Torrence, but I'm sure they will turn out to be the same person. Forensics are looking for anything linking

Torrence to the manipulated brakes on Andrew Campbell's car."

The Super was aghast.

"An attempt on Andrew Campbell's life has already been made?"

"Two, to be precise, sir," McCord said. "We also found poison in his whisky and toiletries."

"Good God!" Gilchrist exclaimed. "What are you doing about it? It doesn't bear thinking if–"

"A protection officer is with Mr Campbell round the clock, the area around the estate is being heavily patrolled, and I have advised Mr Campbell to avoid all outside contact and be extremely careful with what he consumes."

"Bravo," the Super's voice dripped with sarcasm. "Let's recap – four, *four* brutal murders in the past seven months, and the culprit is running rings around us. I am seriously thinking of taking you off the case."

McCord was stunned.

"Sir?"

"I hear that you spend more time with Miss Amy Thornton these days than with your colleagues. People have the impression that she is a member of the police force, which, if I can remind you, she is not! She is a journalist! What if she reveals your incompetence in her flaming magazine? She could make a packet because readers love nothing better than a scandal, and this is a scandal! Have you seen the papers this morning?!"

"With all due respect, sir," McCord butted in, "you more or less ordered me to give Miss Thornton access to the station. And in any case," he added hastily, seeing his superior's face turn purple, "she has been a huge help. It was her who found the video of Kevin Jones, and it was her who realised that Jones and Torrence were the same person. She is as good as a member of the Campbell family now, and she would never do anything to jeopardise the investigation or undermine our standing."

McCord drew a deep breath.

"Well then," Gilchrist said with an unpleasant smile, "maybe I should let *her* run the investigation because by the looks of it, *you* have achieved very little!"

McCord placed the tips of his fingers together in a gesture of wise contemplation.

"I'll give you three days to find this man, or you'll be replaced. That is all for now."

"Sir," McCord said stiffly and left.

* * *

Back in his office, he found Amy and Calderwood deeply immersed in a cosy chat, which did not improve his mood in the slightest.

"Do you have nothing to work on, DC Calderwood?" He snapped. "Like catching a killer? And should you not be at the magazine?" he asked Amy, only a little more gently.

Amy looked up in surprise. "What's the matter with you? Was Gilchrist in a bad mood?"

"You could say that," McCord replied bitterly. "If I don't find Jones in the next three days, I'll be taken off the case."

"What?" Amy and Calderwood exclaimed in unison.

"No way," Amy said, and her face left no doubt that she meant it.

"Then we'll just have to find Jones in three days," Calderwood said. "We have people checking hotels, B&Bs and hostels; I'll see what they have come up with so far. He must be holed up somewhere."

When Calderwood had left the room, Amy laid her hand gently on McCord's.

"Don't worry, we'll get him."

He turned his hand slowly to hold hers. Their eyes met, and they smiled. Somebody rushed along the corridor, and they quickly withdrew their hands, but the smile lingered a little longer.

Chapter 28

John and Amy were going over her meagre article on a spate of Morningside burglaries, when John mildly pointed out that she should maybe spend some more time on the other crimes in the city in order to fill the next edition.

"I'd love to," Amy said, "but if we don't find Jones in the next couple of days, DI McCord will be taken off the case."

"What?"

"His boss thinks he is not making fast enough progress."

"DI McCord saved Andrew's life; did he not tell his boss that?"

"I'm not sure," Amy said. "He is a proud man."

While John was digesting this bit of bad news, his phone rang.

"Good morning, Mama," he said. "Is everything okay?"

Instead of the usual rant, his mother sounded subdued.

"Not really, John."

There was a moment's silence.

"Has something happened to Andrew?" John asked anxiously.

He switched on the speaker phone, so Amy could hear.

"Something is definitely wrong with Andrew," Edith Campbell specified. "I think he is losing his mental faculties."

"Well, the stress is bound to…"

"He refuses to eat or drink anything that was not bought immediately before the meal. I have been backwards and forwards to M&S three times a day. Every time I've had to buy new toiletries as well because he throws them away as soon as they have been left in his room for any length of time. He insists I sack Lucy because he thinks Justin, or Jones, might have got to her somehow. I have refused, of course, but he won't let it go. And this morning" – she swallowed hard as she fought back the tears – "our postman came, you know the one we've had for years, and he sees Andrew, who was outside with the protection officer to get some air, and he tells Andrew that a man he has never seen before was at the post office and asked how Andrew was doing and if he still enjoyed a fine wine. Andrew just turned, ran into the wine cellar and now he's pouring all the wine down the drain! Your dad's wonderful collection! It was worth a fortune, as well. The policeman tried to stop him, but he went berserk, waving a broken bottle at us and shouting, 'I'm just trying to save you all!' Can you not speak to him, John, and make him see reason?"

She began to sob. John had only seen his mother cry once, and that was after his father had died. He looked at Amy in alarm.

"Have you told DI McCord? They need to check out the post office!"

"Of course, I did. But what shall I do about Andrew?"

"Ask Dr Williams to come up immediately. Maybe he can prescribe some tranquillisers. DI McCord has suggested that you and Andrew should leave the estate for the time being, and I agree. It is too difficult to police and too dangerous for all of you. How about moving down south and staying with Aunt Patsy until Jones has been caught?"

There was a silence at the other end. Then the old Edith Campbell was back.

"This estate has been in the family for almost two hundred years," she said firmly. "I'm not going to be chased away by some jumped-up lunatic. We'll get through this."

John looked at Amy and shook his head.

"Then how about sending Andrew abroad for a while?" he suggested. "Don't we have relations in Canada somewhere? If we keep it a secret, Justin, or rather Kevin Jones, will never find him there. Andrew could relax, and as soon as Justin is caught, Andrew can come back."

"That is a brilliant idea!" Edith Campbell sounded more cheerful now. "I'll get in touch with Glenn, my great-nephew, and see what can be arranged."

"You do that, Mama, and let me know. I can make the arrangements for the flight if you like."

"You are a darling," Edith Campbell said. "I don't know what I would do without you."

Amy mouthed the word 'McCord' to John and pointed to the phone. John nodded.

"Unfortunately, we have some concerns here as well, Mama," he said. "Amy's just told me that DI McCord is to be suspended from the case if he does not catch Justin in the next couple of days. And once he is off the case, Amy won't have any access to the investigation. Is that not a shame?"

He waited expectantly.

"A shame?" Edith Campbell exploded. "It is utterly ridiculous! Without DI McCord, Andrew would be dead by now! Just you leave that to me, John; just you leave that to me. I'll sort this out!"

The line went dead.

A little triumphant smile played around John's mouth.

"Well played," Amy said admiringly. "I think McCord's position is safe for now."

"I need to do something about the estate, however," John said, serious again. "Andrew is not well enough to run the place, nor is Mama. I must find somebody to do the job of estate manager, somebody who is above all suspicion, even to Andrew."

"Why not ask your friend Phoebe?" Amy suggested. "She runs an estate like yours and might know of somebody."

John nodded appreciatively. "I'll phone her right now."

* * *

When McCord and Calderwood arrived at Carnethy post office and village shop, the staff, comprising the postmaster, his wife and his daughter, were already assembled. The wife recognised Calderwood from his earlier visit and tutted.

"You never told me you were a policeman," she said accusingly.

"What can you tell us about the man who asked after Andrew Campbell?" McCord asked and pulled out his notebook.

"It was me who was in the shop when he came in," the wife said. "He was an old man, nothing like the man on the wanted posters; that's why I didn't call the police."

"The man we want is very good at disguising himself," McCord said.

The postmaster's wife shook her head.

"No way. He could barely stand up. He bought a bag of sweets and left."

"Any CCTV?" McCord asked, looking round.

"We don't have CCTV," she said apologetically.

"Pity. Did he pay by credit card?"

She shook her head.

"Cash. It was only 99p, you know. He put a pound on the counter and put the penny in the charity box. The cash has been collected since, unfortunately, but the charity box is still here."

She lifted it carefully. "Should be fairly near the top, I reckon."

"Thanks," McCord said again, but feeling they were clutching desperately at very thin straws.

* * *

"Is there a point chasing a guy who is definitely not Jones?" Calderwood asked when they were driving back into the city.

"I bet you it was him," McCord said.

"But why did he do it?" Calderwood wondered. "It doesn't help him kill Andrew Campbell."

"It doesn't," McCord agreed, "but his question about the wine scared Andrew Campbell senseless and tied up our time and resources. And I'm beginning to wonder if our killer just enjoys playing games."

Chapter 29

"What the hell is this?"

McCord slammed the latest copy of *The Morning Herald* on Calderwood's desk. 'ROCK KILLER TARGET ABOUT TO HIDE ABROAD!' the headline screamed.

"Read on," McCord ordered, his voice barely audible.

Calderwood, who was deathly pale and had winced at the loud bang, slowly pulled the paper towards him.

"'Sources close to the case have revealed that the heir to Carnethy Estate, Andrew Campbell, is travelling to an undisclosed destination abroad in the next few days to escape the Rock Killer, who has already made several attempts to kill him.'"

"How the hell did this get into the papers?" McCord asked again.

"I don't know," Calderwood whispered, looking as if he was going to be sick.

"Amy has just phoned asking me the same question. John and Mrs Campbell swear that that they did not breathe a word to anybody about the flight. Only five people knew about the plan, and I didn't mention it to anybody either. If my maths is correct, that leaves only you. Where were you last night?"

"Out for a drink. Is that not allowed anymore?" Calderwood said, making a misguided attempt at stroppiness.

"More than one drink, judging by your looks this morning," McCord said. "Talk to anybody at all?"

"Just a girl out for a good time. She challenged me to a drinking contest, and by God, she could put it away."

"You didn't by any chance try to impress her by telling her you were involved in the Rock Killer case?"

Calderwood swallowed.

"I might have done. To be honest, I don't remember much about last night."

McCord smiled mirthlessly.

"Is her name one of the things you do remember? Was it Ruth, by any chance?"

His finger stabbed the flimsy paper below the by-line of the article. "Ruth McCowan, maybe?"

"Oh my God," Calderwood moaned and covered his face with his hands.

A PC appeared at the door.

"Yes?" McCord snapped. "What is it?"

"Superintendent Gilchrist wants to see you both. Now, he said." Having delivered her message, she hastily withdrew.

McCord took a deep breath.

"Well then, come on," he ordered Calderwood. "And pull yourself together, man."

Gilchrist was pacing up and down his office, waving an edition of *The Morning Herald* at the detectives as they entered. His face displayed the other end of the scale of skin colour to Calderwood's ashen complexion, and McCord wondered if he was predestined for a stroke. Now would be a good time, he thought, but they weren't so lucky.

"I don't know what to do with you, DI McCord," he fumed. "I learn from *The Morning Herald – The Morning Herald!* – that the man we are protecting from the Rock Killer is about to leave the country! Why was I not informed? And who has leaked this to the gutter press?"

McCord sensed Calderwood's panic and answered quickly.

"We tried to keep the number of people who know very limited but there is always the possibility that the press finds out. One careless remark is enough now that everybody is talking about the case. You know what the papers pay for a story. As it happens," he quickly carried on before the Super could interrupt, "this might work to our advantage."

"And how is that?" Gilchrist enquired with his usual sarcasm where McCord's plans were involved.

"Andrew Campbell is Jones's only target. Once he is out of the country, Jones will find it very difficult to get to him. So, now he is under pressure. He only has a couple of days to get to Andrew Campbell, and we will be ready for him. This is the only way to bring this sorry tale to an end once and for all."

Gilchrist needed a minute to process the implications of McCord's words, and, judging by his face, he did not like them.

"If it were down to me, you would be out on your ear, DI McCord, but for some unfathomable reason, you seem to have friends in high places. The assistant chief constable has intervened on your behalf and told me to keep you on the case. Well, you'd better make sure that it all works out!"

He waved them away, like some irritating insects, and pointedly threw the paper in the bin.

McCord and Calderwood exited quickly before their boss could think of anything else to say.

Out in the corridor, Calderwood exhaled with relief.

"Thank you, sir," he said quietly. "I swear, I'll never let you down like that again."

McCord just nodded impatiently and motioned him back into the office. They had to prepare for Jones's final attack.

* * *

John's friend Phoebe Smythe-Tennison had been as good as her word and sent over Craig Fletcher, her own assistant estate manager, who had grown up on her estate and was looking for a promotion. John was not sure where the money for the man's salary would come from, but Phoebe assured him that he was full of energy and good ideas and, once the scandal surrounding the estate had died down, he would find ways to generate money from the estate that would pay his wages many times over. Craig Fletcher was quite excited by the prospect of hunting a killer on the estate, but John urged caution and gave him his and McCord's mobile numbers in case he noticed anything unusual.

John did not expect, however, to hear from Craig Fletcher quite so soon.

"Mr Campbell," the young man said breathlessly through a crackling line, "I've been patrolling the estate, and guess what I found just now."

"Do tell," John said, ever polite.

"Remnants of a campfire on the western side. Still warm. And whoever was there, left a note."

"What does it say?"

"'Still alive – well done. But it was in vain: prepare to die a thousand deaths.'"

"Dear God," John said. "Phone DI McCord immediately and don't touch anything. Then go back to the house and help the protection officer guard my brother. Oh, and don't tell him about this, only my mother. I'll be up as soon as I can."

"Yes, Mr Campbell," Craig Fletcher said. "On my way."

* * *

When John and Amy arrived at Carnethy House, Craig Fletcher was patrolling the outside of the house, carrying a rifle. Andrew had locked himself in his room with two guns and a couple of boxes of cartridges. The protection officer stood guard outside the room and motioned to John and Amy to stay clear of the door. John was about to ask why, when Amy pointed out the bullet hole in the middle of the door.

"He overheard Fletcher tell me about the campfire and the note," Edith Campbell said. "The window was open."

Andrew was shouting through the door, swearing at an imaginary Jones and promising that he would get him first.

"DI McCord is sending reinforcements," the officer told John, politely omitting the fact that they would not just be protecting Andrew from Jones, but also the rest of the household from Andrew.

When her son grew tired of ranting, Edith Campbell took the opportunity to intervene.

"Andrew, darling, please take one of the Valium capsules that Dr Williams gave you. Just one for now. Are you listening to me, Andrew?"

"I don't want Valium," Andrew whined, suddenly sounding broken. "I want Jones to be dead."

"Don't we all," mumbled the protection officer. "I don't know how long this can go on."

John exchanged a look with Amy. Andrew would be flying to Canada the following day. All they had to do was to hang on for twenty-four hours.

Chapter 30

As McCord climbed the stairs up to the main entrance of Carnethy House, he thought about the note left at the campfire.

> *Still alive – well done. But it was in vain: prepare to die a thousand deaths.*

Jones was mocking them, not just Andrew, but also him.

Irritably, he passed the officer guarding the door and went straight into the drawing room where the family was assembled having tea and sandwiches.

"Please take a seat, DI McCord, and have some refreshments," Edith Campbell said. "You must be exhausted."

McCord shook his head.

"Thank you, but I must be on my way. Have you told Andrew about tomorrow?"

"We did, but it made matters worse," John Campbell said. "He is even more anxious now that Jones has only hours left."

McCord nodded.

"Understandable, but by this time tomorrow, he will be thirty thousand feet in the air, and this nightmare will be over."

* * *

Back at St Leonard's, McCord ordered another full-scale search of Carnethy House and ten police officers to guard the house until Andrew Campbell's plane would be in the air. The journey they would take to the airport had been meticulously planned; he and John would accompany Andrew to the door of the plane. DC Sutton was double-checking the passenger list, just in case, and two officers had been assigned to supervise the check-in process. Calderwood had cautiously voiced his concern that his boss was developing a certain degree of paranoia himself, but McCord, who explained the deployment of all these resources to a bad-tempered Gilchrist, was determined to get Andrew safely out of the country.

He had even accepted Mrs Campbell's offer of staying overnight to save him coming back in the morning. Amy was staying in George Street to keep her mother company while John also spent the night at Carnethy House.

The evening dragged on in strained conversation. Mrs Campbell had tried to coax Andrew out of his room for dinner, but he had shouted through the door that Jones only had a few hours left to get him, and he was not going take a chance.

They retired early. McCord waited for the hand-over to the protection officer for the night shift, an experienced and reliable colleague, and after checking the perimeter of the house one more time, he went to his room. Upon his request, it was in the same corridor as Andrew's.

He nodded off briefly in the early hours after reading the latest RSPB magazine from cover to cover but woke up around 4am when a tawny owl started hooting somewhere outside. He got up and scanned the black silhouette of a larch for the outline of the bird but could not make it out. He could not see any of the guards either, and was just about to get dressed and check, when one of the officers slowly sauntered across the gravel. Each of his steps seemed to echo through the whole estate. McCord shivered due to the draught coming through the old sash window, and quickly crawled back into his warm bed.

* * *

It was a relief when morning came. Andrew's cases, packed by Mrs Campbell herself, stood ready in the hall. At eight, the family sat down to a sumptuous breakfast. John had driven to the baker's in Carnethy, but even warm croissants and fluffy morning rolls filled with bacon could not tempt Andrew to join them.

"Don't you understand, there are only a few hours left?" Andrew had shouted at his mother through the door of his room.

"He could at least have come out to have a last meal with us before he leaves," Edith Campbell said bitterly. "His father would not have hidden in his room, whining; he would have shown some backbone. I don't think Andrew accepts any degree of responsibility for what is happening here; everything is always about Andrew Campbell. I've spoilt him too much, haven't I?"

McCord examined his plate, determined not to answer, and kept checking his watch.

"The taxi is late," he said, trying not to let his nerves show.

A few minutes later, they heard the honking of a horn outside.

"That must be it," McCord said. "Better late than never, I suppose. Thank you for the breakfast. Mrs Campbell, could you fetch Andrew, please?"

Edith Campbell nodded and went off to coax her son out of his room. John followed McCord outside where a taxi was pulling up in front of the stone steps.

"I tried to get a police car, but Superintendent Gilchrist said the police are not a taxi service, and heaven forbid *The Morning Herald* would get wind of the fact that the taxpayer's money was used to ferry the landed gentry around. Sorry."

John waved his apology away. "We know you could not have done any more," he said. "Oh, DC Calderwood is here too."

True enough, Calderwood's Mondeo was already sitting in the driveway.

"You and I will be with Andrew in the taxi, and DC Calderwood is going to follow us in his car," McCord explained. "That way we have backup in any emergency, and he can take us home again afterwards."

John nodded, looking relieved.

"You have thought of everything, DI McCord."

"I hope so."

The taxi driver, a middle-aged man with the bulging waistline often seen in people who spend their lives behind the wheel, heaved himself out of the driver's seat, looking around for his clients.

"You're late," McCord remarked curtly.

"I underestimated the time it would take me to get out here, and then I was stopped by a mob of reporters at the gate. I could hardly mow them down."

McCord mumbled something unintelligible.

"You are late," a voice echoed McCord's complaint from the top of the stairs. "Why are you late?"

Andrew Campbell slowly descended the stairs, staggering under the weight of two large, heavy suitcases. McCord was shocked to see the change in John's brother. Ghastly pale, thin and feverishly tense, his eyes darted around him as if he expected Jones to jump up from behind the house, the trees and the people standing around.

The taxi driver moved forward. "I'll help you with the luggage, sir."

It was more a statement than an offer, and Andrew Campbell recoiled.

"Nobody touches my stuff. I'll do it myself."

"Please yourself," the driver said, his face impassive.

He opened the boot of the car as Andrew put one suitcase down and lifted the other up to the rim.

"Hang on," the driver said, bending down. "I'll move the jack. I had to change a tyre yesterday and haven't got round to putting it back."

With a sudden scream, Andrew dropped the case, wrenched the jack from the driver's hand and brought it down on his head.

"It's you," he yelled, lifting the jack to land another blow, "it's you!"

In a flash, Calderwood jumped forward and grabbed Andrew's arm, not quite fast enough to stop the second blow but to divert it from the driver's head onto his shoulder. McCord grabbed Andrew's other arm, and together they wrestled him to the ground.

"Stop," McCord gasped, "are you crazy? Stop!"

"It's him!" Andrew shouted. "Can't you see? It was his last chance to get me! Let me go, I need to make sure he's dead!"

Calderwood exchanged a glance with McCord, who nodded. Calderwood twisted the struggling man's arms and, with a knee on his back, handcuffed him. McCord scrambled to his feet. John stood next to the taxi, his face white. He was trying to call an ambulance, his hands shaking.

McCord moved closer to the still figure of the taxi driver, whose upper body was leaning into the boot. His head was covered in blood. McCord felt for a pulse.

"He's alive. There must be a first-aid kit in the taxi," he told Edith Campbell, who was just standing there, clearly in shock. "Quickly, please!"

Jolted out of her stupor, she dived under the passenger seat and emerged with a green pouch. McCord grabbed a packet of bandages, tore the wrapping off and pressed them onto the head wound.

Edith Campbell stared first at her prostrate son, who was still screaming threats to kill Jones, then at the half-hidden figure of the driver.

"Get us a blanket, Mrs Campbell," McCord commanded. "Everything will be fine. Just get us a blanket."

She hurried into the house and came back seconds later with an armful of blankets and a cushion.

With trembling hands, she laid them out on the gravel. John had finished the call and helped McCord to lay the injured man on the ground. The bandages were soaked in blood, and John ran into the house to get some more.

Calderwood was still trying to hold a frantic Andrew Campbell down, whose shouting had subsided into sobs.

"He was trying to kill me, he was trying to kill me," he repeated endlessly.

His mother knelt beside him, tears running down her face.

"Andrew, Andrew, listen to me, listen. Nobody is trying to kill you. He is just the taxi driver."

Andrew closed his eyes in despair.

"Can you not see it, Mama? It is him!"

"Look at him, Andrew," she urged him. "He is at least fifty and weighs 200 pounds!"

"It is easy to make yourself look older. Actors do it all the time. And he's wearing padding round his waist, I'll show you!"

Calderwood held him down even harder. The gravel scraped Andrew's face, leaving long, red marks as if he had been clawed.

"Lie still, Mr Campbell," he said. "I don't want to hurt you, but you must calm down."

Eventually, Andrew Campbell's strength was exhausted. Calderwood helped him up into a sitting position with his back resting on the wheel of the taxi. His head swung from side to side in obstinate denial. There was a soft moan from the driver, who had regained consciousness. Andrew Campbell began to struggle again.

"He's waking up, he's not dead! DI McCord, you have to arrest him!"

"Where is that goddamn ambulance?" McCord muttered through his teeth, pressing a fresh roll of bandages to the driver's head. He listened for the hum of an engine but all he could hear was the mewing of a buzzard circling above. It sounded like Kevin Jones's laughter.

Chapter 31

The front of Carnethy House was eerily quiet. A wailing ambulance had taken the injured taxi driver away, followed by Calderwood, who was going to inform his family and employer. A second ambulance was on its way to the Royal Edinburgh Hospital where Andrew's mental state would be assessed before he was charged.

John had accompanied his brother and promised to keep the family and McCord up to date. All other police cars but one had left for Edinburgh, and only a couple of officers were patrolling the outside of the building where Mrs Campbell had retired, accompanied by Craig Fletcher.

McCord stood alone on the stone steps, taking in the abandoned taxi and the churned up pink gravel that had lost its lustre now the sky had thrown a grey, suffocating blanket over the land. McCord's blood had turned to lead, and if Jones turned up now with a rock in his hand, he would have nothing left to fight him. He did not even have the strength to go inside and face the brittle figure of Edith Campbell, who seemed to have visibly shrunk after her ordeal. What a fool he had been! Jones had achieved exactly what he wanted without lifting a finger against Andrew Campbell, who had escaped jail only to be imprisoned in a secure psychiatric unit. Jones's last note came to mind again, and only now did McCord understand the second half of it. Andrew Campbell was dying a thousand deaths; dying every time he scrutinized a new face, looking for the slate grey eyes and a thin white scar on a wrist. McCord shivered.

Scanning the horizon, he noticed a little dot in the distance, slowly and slightly erratically moving along the driveway towards the house. Puzzled, he followed its progress until he could make out what it was. Relieved, he recognised Lucy, struggling up the hill on her bike. She dismounted before the gravel made her progress impossible and leant her bike against the low, curved wall separating the house from the wilderness beyond.

"What is going on?" she shouted at McCord from ten yards away. "The people in the village say two ambulances and lots of police cars came from here, and all the reporters were following them. Justin didn't come back and attack Mr Campbell, did he?"

"No, he didn't," McCord said heavily. He looked at her closely. "Mr Campbell has been taken to hospital. I suppose you are not too unhappy that he may be gone some time?"

Lucy held his gaze. "I am not," she confirmed.

"What happened to you after you started working here?" McCord asked.

Lucy bit her lip.

"Campbell and his chums thought it would be fun to have a bit of a gang bang with the servant," she spat. "I suppose I was lucky that I had some fight in me, and when they realised I would not lie down quietly, they gave up."

"And despite this, you stayed?" McCord said.

"Campbell pretended that nothing had happened, and I was quite sure he would not try anything again. I needed the job, but I also grew to like Justin. He was the opposite of Campbell, in a way. I always felt safe with him. Ironic, isn't it?"

"Indeed," McCord said. "Why don't you go inside and look after Mrs Campbell? She is not feeling very well, and you'll find her a little more appreciative, I think," he said.

Nodding, Lucy hurried up the steps and into the house.

McCord gazed out over the empty, rolling hills. As soon as he had written his report, he would take a couple of days off and go birdwatching. Not here, in the Pentlands, where everything reminded him of Jones, no, somewhere quite different, somewhere on the coast where the waders had arrived. He would analyse flight patterns, identify calls and lose himself in the contemplation of these creatures who, despite being so delicate and vulnerable, had survived since the time of the dinosaurs. Every autumn he was touched again by those intrepid migrants who arrived after flying thousands of miles to escape the arctic winter, only to make the return journey in the spring.

The purring of an engine in the distance jolted him out of his reverie. Who was that now? It had better not be the press, he thought. His heart made a little leap when he recognised Valerie's dark blue MG, and somersaulted when it was Amy who pulled up next to him. It was the press, after all, but the best kind.

She slid out of the low seat with her usual grace and did not even wobble when her heels tried to get a hold in the gravel.

"I heard what's happened," she told McCord. "Mum's gone off to be with John, and I thought you could do with some backup here."

She opened the passenger seat, pulled out two large shopping bags and dropped them heavily to the ground.

McCord was still standing there, rooted to the spot.

"Are you going to watch me hauling them up the stairs or are you going to help?" she mockingly called up to him.

Finally, his blood was flowing freely again. He bounced down the steps and picked up the bags.

"What is all this?" he asked.

"Lunch and tea," she said. "I just thought Edith Campbell might have too much on her mind to be thinking about food."

"And there was me thinking you are just after an exclusive."

Amy smiled and tapped her nose.

"You know me too well. Need to keep ahead of the pack. Can't have the servants talk to the gutter press, can we?"

She walked up the steps ahead of him, and he almost stumbled over the wonky step halfway up admiring her slightly swinging hips.

* * *

"Of course, there will be an internal inquiry into this whole shambolic investigation," Superintendent Gilchrist announced grimly a few days later. "If you remember, I told you that Andrew Campbell was innocent from the beginning. But you refused to see the obvious. I suspect it can be explained by your background and upbringing; explained, mind you, not excused. Social prejudice does not behove a senior police officer, DI McCord. You are due some leave; I suggest you take it, while another officer takes over the hunt for Jones and tries to salvage what can be salvaged, if indeed anything can be salvaged from this unmitigated disaster. Also, you will be attending a training course on equality and inclusion where you will have the opportunity to examine your attitude to authority. And I doubt," he added with barely concealed glee, "that the assistant chief constable will be intervening on your behalf this time."

The only reason McCord did not punch Gilchrist at this point was the memory of the blood seeping out of the taxi driver's skull and Andrew Campbell's agonised screams that haunted his dreams. Gilchrist's words, no matter how unfair the accusations, only echoed his own sense of utter failure. The taxi driver was still in hospital suffering from localised brain damage which, according to the doctors, could be permanent, and from what John was saying, Andrew's paranoia showed no sign of abating. Worst of all, he had not the slightest clue as to where Jones was hiding and not a shred of evidence to link him to any of the crimes.

"Are we done here, sir?" McCord asked with gritted teeth.

"For now," Gilchrist said sternly. "For now."

* * *

Back in his office, Calderwood and Amy were waiting nervously for his return.

"And?" Amy demanded when, without saying a word, McCord began to tidy his desk, leaving the five files documenting his failure neatly stacked in the centre for his replacement.

"On leave pending an internal inquiry," he said eventually, summarising the verdict. "Somebody else is taking over the case. Cheer up, Calderwood," he said, seeing the DC's stricken face, "at least you'll have a boss you can discuss cricket with."

"It is ridiculous," Amy blustered. "You did nothing wrong. Jones was so twisted and clever, nobody could have prevented all this."

"Exactly," Calderwood said. "I'm sure the inquiry will come to the same conclusion. I hear Mrs Campbell has already started a campaign on your behalf. And I'll look after your azalea while you're away; at least now it has a chance to recover."

McCord gave a half smile.

"Oh, before I forget, while you were with the Super, a letter came for you, from Germany."

"Germany?" McCord looked closely at the stamp. The Brandenburg Gate. "I don't know anybody in Germany as far as I know."

He tore open the envelope and pulled out a postcard. It showed a black-and-white woodcut depicting an angel casting a dragon into a hole in the ground. A sudden chill ran down McCord's spine. He turned over the card.

"'The Angel with the Key to the Bottomless Pit by Albrecht Dürer'," he read the caption aloud and looked up, puzzled.

"The Book of Revelation," Calderwood explained. "We did that at school in religious studies once. The angel throws Satan and all the bad guys into the fire for a thousand years until Christ comes back for Judgement Day. I'm sure it was an attempt by our chaplain to keep us on the straight and narrow."

"What else does it say?" Amy asked impatiently. By now she knew who it was from.

McCord cleared his throat.

"'Despite your best efforts, justice has been done. You are a good man, DI McCord, and I hope, like me, you'll find peace.'"

Calderwood jumped up.

"I'll take it to the lab. Maybe there is DNA on it!"

"There won't be," McCord said, dropping the card into an evidence bag. "But I suppose we have to go through the motions. I'm sorry, Calderwood, I had hoped our first case together would end in an arrest. But at least we found out the truth."

Amy watched him put on his jacket.

"Where are you going?" she asked.

"Bird watching." There was a brief hesitation. "Want to join me?"

She shook her head regretfully.

"The weekend edition, you know–"

"Of course," he interrupted her hastily. "It would probably bore you to death anyway."

Before she could protest, he added, "Don't worry, once I've had my knuckles rapped, I'll be back."

List of characters

Police

Detective Inspector Russell McCord
Superintendent Gilchrist
DC Duncan Calderwood
Jack – Duty Sergeant
Dr Crane – pathologist
DC Heather 'The Hacker' Sutton

Others

Amy Thornton – fashion journalist at the *Forth Write* magazine
Valerie Thornton – Amy's mother
Martin Eden – Amy's colleague
John Campbell – owner of *Forth Write*
Edith Campbell – John's mother
Andrew Campbell – John's brother
Lucy – housekeeper
Justin Torrence – estate manager
Jordan Lamond – victim
Michael Sloan – Lamond's colleague
Robert 'Robbie' McArthur – victim
Eilidh Gordon – witness
Olivia McArthur – victim's wife
Zacharias Walker – member of 'The Players'
Alex Buchan – member of 'The Players'

Cheryl Gibbs, neé Langley – old friend of 'The Players'
William Gibbs – Cheryl's husband
Alan Cooper – Campbell's lawyer
Craig Fletcher – assistant estate manager

If you enjoyed this book, please let others know by leaving a quick review on Amazon. Also, if you spot anything untoward in the paperback, get in touch. We strive for the best quality and appreciate reader feedback.

editor@thebookfolks.com

Also by Traude Ailinger

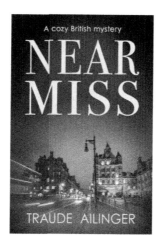

NEAR MISS (book 1)

After being nearly hit by a car, fashion journalist Amy
Thornton decides to visit the driver, who ends up in
hospital after evading her. Curious about this strange
man she becomes convinced she's unveiled a murder
plot. But it won't be so easy to persuade Scottish
detective DI Russell McCord.

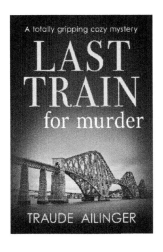

LAST TRAIN FOR MURDER (book 3)

An investigative journalist who made a career out of sticking it to the man dies on a train to Edinburgh, having been poisoned. DI Russell McCord struggles in the investigation after getting banned from contacting helpful but self-serving reporter Amy Thornton. But the latter is ready to go in, all guns blazing. After the smoke has cleared, what will remain standing?

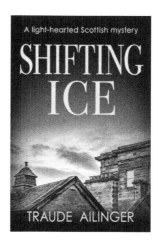

A light-hearted Scottish mystery

SHIFTING ICE

TRAUDE AILINGER

SHIFTING ICE (book 4)

After a jewellery thief meets a bitter end, DI McCord
tries to make sense of his dying words. Are they a clue
to his killer? He'll find out. Meanwhile journalist Amy
Thornton is forbidden from taking on dangerous
investigations, and sent on a fool's errand. Hmmm.
She'll wiggle out of just about anything. Except perhaps
the place she might hold in the cop's heart.

Other titles of interest

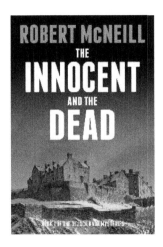

THE INNOCENT AND THE DEAD by Robert McNeill

One girl is found dead – strangled in the woods. Another, the daughter of a rich, well-connected businessman, is kidnapped. Unassuming detective, Jack Knox, must solve these two cases. But the Edinburgh crime-solver will have a hard time getting his superiors to accept his unconventional methods. Will he gamble too much?

NO REFUGE by Nicola Clifford

Reporter Stacey Logan has little to worry about other than the town flower festival when a man is shot dead. When she believes the police have got the wrong man, she does some snooping of her own. But will her desire for a scoop lead her to a place where there is no refuge?

Sign up to our mailing list to find out about new releases and special offers!

www.thebookfolks.com